2035

REVELATION

Mark's story

The Steel Wheels of The Winds of Change

by

Freddy Campbell

Grosvenor House
Publishing Limited

The right of Freddy Campbell to be identified as the author of this
work has been asserted in accordance with Section 78
of the Copyright, Designs and Patents Act 1988

The book cover picture is copyright Imogen Campbell 2016

This book is published by
Grosvenor House Publishing Ltd
28-30 High Street, Guildford, Surrey, GU1 3EL.
www.grosvenorhousepublishing.co.uk

This is a work of fiction. Names, characters, incidents and places
are used fictitiously. Any resemblance to actual people, living or dead,
organisations, events or locations is entirely coincidental.

A CIP record for this book
is available from the British Library

ISBN 978-1-78623-014-0

For my children
I love you love you love you.

What follows is imagined.
However, similar things have
happened in the past.

DAY ONE

In a large dormitory, in a megacity in Southern England, a Level Three Worker was sound asleep, like all the others in his unit.

Except unlike all the others, he was dreaming.

He was standing in bright sunshine, looking across sand dunes at a sight which was at the same time the most frightening, exciting, awesome, and spectacular thing that he had ever laid eyes on. It was so tall he could not see the top of it. It reached way up into the sky. The body of it was dark brown, like the colour of dark brown sugar, and moving. As he looked more closely, he could see that there were great violent whirls of brown sand and dirt. The sand was churning and swirling at high speed. It was an enormous sandstorm moving across his view. It was huge and violent and nothing like he had ever experienced. Something about the base of it drew his attention. At ground level, there seemed to be things like huge discs turning. They looked like huge round saws, the height of a house, spinning with blurring speed. He could tell from their colour and glint that they were steel. He could see that they would destroy anything in their path. The storm was some distance away so that all he could hear was the rushing sound of the wind. It was the most terrible thing he had ever seen.

Words came into his mind: *The steel wheels of the winds of change.*

He woke up, together with all the others in the dormitory, when three loud notes were sounded for Rise. The notes were not as harsh as an alarm bell, but they had the same effect. For a moment, he blinked, glancing briefly around the space. Everything was familiar: the ceiling was light and high; the walls were plain and unadorned; lines of beds stretched in every direction. As he stood, the floor was cool and hard. Everyone was standing to attention next to their beds, ready for the notes to sound for them to file off to the washrooms and lockers to shower and climb into their day kit. There were Supervisors watching them.

His head had a centimetre of hair, like all the others. He was dressed in his night kit, like the rest. If you looked along the rows, there was little to distinguish one male from the next except some physical features - height, build, and skin colour. His identification number and dot code were printed on a panel on the breast of his top: G1L3E290718RN052CBS4U BWM4C.

This stood for Generation 1; Level 3; Europe; 29 July 2018; Register Number 052; City B, Sector 4, Unit Block West M; Floor 4; Room C.

Another set of notes sounded and the lines of young men marched towards the lockers beside the washroom. He pulled off his night gear, took his turn in the shower and dressed. Day gear consisted of a grey collarless shirt, a dull blue top, matching blue trousers and boots. His number and code were sown in the same place on his breast and his unit number was stenciled in large lettering across his back.

He stood again, waiting for the next notes to sound to signal the group to move off from the lockers, and file downstairs and across the street towards the canteen block. The climate of the street was comfortable because it was roofed at high level, like a high atrium.

The canteen served one thousand men, but he knew exactly where to walk, where to collect his morning meal and where to sit. He took his portion: two slaps of hot porridge with a slurry of cooked fruit, a mug of hot, milky tea and a muffin. They did this every morning; it was routine. There were precious few words spoken - there was the occasional bark from a Supervisor. No one showed any emotion. They listened to the Morning Music while they ate, until the notes that sounded at the beginning of Morning Announcements. By now, everyone had finished eating and drinking.

There on the screens was the face of the Announcer.

"Good morning, Workers. Today, it is Day 6494 and we can announce that the target for carbon neutrality for last year has been achieved. The world is now fifty-two per cent carbon neutral! We have achieved this through our work together. Our world working population is now four billion seven hundred and fifty-three million, four hundred and twenty-two thousand, eight hundred."

The Announcer read some more facts and news items then, when the notes sounded, every Worker picked up his tray and moved along to the clearing area and then to the rows of information screens.

When it was his turn, he placed his hand over the scanner screen. An electronic voice spoke his identity number and then said,

"Today you will work in Observation Room 412 until lunch, then you will work in Laundry Room 134 until dinner."

He headed along a wide route to the Observation complex, passing countless other men. He walked to the bank of lifts and went up to Level 4. Workers in similar outfits moved to their workstations. The corridors and lift lobbies were busy on every floor. He found Room 412 easily from the huge number on the door. He had worked on this level many times before. He filed in and registered with the Supervisors. They were dressed in black. Many of them were older. A Supervisor pointed to a workstation. He went over and logged in. He read the instructions that came up. He was to observe units in Zone A. Down the sides of the centre screen there were smaller displays. If he touched one of them, they filled the centre display area. He had a menu to add different displays.

The notes sounded for the work to begin. He settled down to watch Workers on factory assembly lines, in laundry rooms, in kitchens, on construction sites, in canteens and in storage depots. There was a multitude of activities, but nothing surprised him. He had done this many times before. If there was anything that seemed incorrect, he could zoom in on the individual concerned. If the person seemed to be doing something that was questionable, he could drag an alert tag onto that person. The alert would be picked up by one of the Supervisors. They worked on the central bank of terminals on the raised area in the centre of the room. There was no conversation, only the sounds of people working, and the Morning Music coming from the speakers in the ceiling.

After about an hour, he spotted a bulldozer driver on a construction site who was not moving. He zoomed in to observe more closely. It looked like the driver was slumped at the wheel. He concluded that he must be asleep in the cab. He waited two minutes but the man did move and so he placed the alert tag on the man. He carried on surveying other scenes. He worked without any sign of interest in the subjects of his observation. All around the room, men of the same age were doing exactly as he did. They worked quietly and methodically.

Their expressions did not change. If you studied their faces closely, you could not detect any emotion.

Occasionally, someone would get up, motion to his Supervisor and head to the toilets up the corridor. A trolley arrived from the canteen with tea and a snack.

There was a tap on his shoulder. Two Supervisors were looking down at him through narrowed eyes.

"Come with me," said one of them.

He marched the Worker along to the bank of lifts. They went up to an upper floor and along a corridor to a door marked 601.

The room was brightly lit. He was told to sit in a chair.

Another Supervisor entered.

"Hold still," commanded the man.

He held a device and scanned one eye then inspected the device.

"Anything different last night when you were asleep?"

The question was delivered like a blow.

The Worker shook his head.

The two men stood back and compared devices. They nodded agreement.

One of the devices showed his file. It read 'fear of heights.'

The door opened and a third man entered. He wore black clothes.

He came over to the Worker, gripped his shoulder and pulled him to his feet. He took the Worker along the corridor to another room marked 606.

"In this room, you are mine," said the man. "I can do to you whatever I like."

He picked up a whip and brought it down on the table, making the Worker jump. Then he took a cord and bound it around the Worker's neck.

Holding one end, he pulled him to the open window. He thrust the Worker's upper body into the opening. The Worker was looking straight down at the hard surface of the street below with the cord tight around his neck.

"Now you listen: you have anything to report, you report it to the first Supervisor you see. Got it?"

He yanked the Worker back up onto his feet. "You got it?"

The Worker nodded, face pale, eyes wide, hands shaking.

The man removed the cord and, holding his shoulder in a grip like a vice, took him back to the Supervisors in Room 601.

The Worker was marched back to Room 412 and told to continue observations.

Notes sounded for the end of the session and he returned to the canteen for lunch.

After the meal he filed in the line for the banks of information screens to confirm his directions for the afternoon session.

"You will work in Laundry Room 134 until dinner," the voice told him.

He headed along a wide concrete street. The buildings were many storeys high above him. The atrium roof allowed sunlight to filter down onto the concrete walls. The air was conditioned and there was only movement of air when he passed a ventilation outlet.

On his way to another section, he passed men dressed in the same uniform, walking unhurriedly to their next assignments.

He found the Laundry room on the first floor. It was a similar size to the canteen. It was laid out in a very orderly way: on one side of the room, there were stacks of washing in large bins divided into sections, each for one unit of one hundred Workers; there were rows of industrial size washing machines then ranks of dryer machines and tables for ironing.

He registered with a Supervisor and took his place at one of the tables. With four other Workers, he spread out clothes and they used the controller to bring down the ironing slab to press them. Another team of Workers collected the pressed and folded clothes in wheeled bins and moved them to the storage area so that they would be ready to be taken to the lockers in the dormitory blocks. As they completed one lot of laundry, men from another team brought over baskets of dried laundry that were ready for pressing. Everyone seemed to know his role so the process seemed to work like clockwork. There was no conversation, just the occasional nod or gesture. There was a rhythm to their work. The gushing steam, as they brought down the press, sounded above the hum of the machines in the washing section.

They all halted when they heard the loud notes and gathered around the canteen trolleys for the afternoon snack. No one had a watch because there were always the notes to start and stop the session.

They kept up their work until the notes sounded again to signal the end of the session. They switched off the machines and headed for the exit when the Supervisors had checked all was correct at their table.

He made his way back to his unit Rec Room, where there were men using the information screens and browsing pages on news from the Executive, or news from other sections. Most of the men were sitting and watching the large screens where the Announcer was introducing news stories from around the world. There was a report on the wolf population in some distant forests. There was another report on the marine life of an ocean reef. He touched the information screens and found that his next session was fitness. He made his way to the exercise gym and registered with a Supervisor then joined many others in a rotation of individual exercises.

When he had completed his circuit, he checked out with the Supervisor and went to shower in the washrooms. He placed his dirty clothes in one of the trolley bins and found new clothes in his locker. He returned to the information area and the notes soon sounded to direct them to move to the canteen block for dinner.

He had the same food as the rest of his unit. Tonight, they had a bowl of tomato soup, a plate of couscous with a sauce of vegetables and a few pieces of chicken, followed by a plain raisin cake. They ate in silence while the Evening Announcements played. He had shut out the memory of the dream and so he had not thought about it all day.

After dinner, he returned to the Rec Room with his unit. On the screens, there was a speech from one of the leaders of the New Order. He did not recognise him. They all sat and listened. There were exactly one hundred young men. They were all close in age. They were all seventeen years old and they were all born between the first day of July and the last day of September in the year 2018. They did not know this. None of them knew the day of their birth. They did not know that the date that day was the 12th April 2035. He sat and listened like all the others. He was totally unaware that he would come to remember this day as the last day before everything changed for him.

The speech ended and the Announcer bid them a good night. He got up and walked to the washrooms to brush his teeth, and then to the locker-room to get into his nightclothes. He found his bed among the neat lines, ten by ten. His was near the middle: row six, bed number five. He lay down and closed his eyes.

Soon the note sounded. The lights were turned off and the Supervisors left. Silently, from small outlets under every bed, there issued a clear gas. Within minutes, all of them were asleep.

His sleep was normally empty of anything visual. It was like passing into a warm fog, without any sound or sight, and with no feeling.

The hours passed.

Workers in identical dormitories were asleep: the men in their sectors, the women in theirs. Recorded voices of a man and a woman gave the Night-time Messages: the kind of words a mother or a father would say to comfort a child. There were Supervisors on night shifts, keeping watch from Observation Rooms, but otherwise the whole city slept.

Suddenly, he came out of the fog and into a dream:

He was standing in bright sunshine, shading his eyes from the intense glare. It took moments for him to focus. The air was hot and dry in his nostrils. He was looking at the sandstorm in all its vivid colour and movement. He felt the same shudder, seeing something so vast and terrible. The steel wheels were spinning at its base like giant saws. The vision was exactly the same as before.

But this time, a voice next to him said:

"Mark."

He turned to find a man of about the same age, standing next to him. He looked into his eyes.

"You are being called," the man said, "it is time for you to wake up."

* * * * * *

Flashback Saturday 17th January 1953

The rain was falling steadily through the central London smog. Looking down on Pall Mall, the black taxis plied their trade and a few people on foot moved to and fro in the street-lit darkness. Four black umbrellas emerged from the Royal Motoring Club and moved West along the pavement. They headed past St. James's Palace and turned up the hill to an ornate entrance on the East side of St. James's Street. Entering Grey's Club, the four men left their overcoats and umbrellas with the cloakroom attendants and mounted the stairs. They were elegantly dressed in tailcoats, as was customary for a high society wedding. They all wore the same old school tie. They each carried the confident air of someone who has known privilege since birth.

In the dining room, they were shown to a table in the far corner. Some of the other diners only glanced in their direction. An old general with a white moustache stared disapprovingly at the Indian.

They devoured their dinner, chatting like close friends do, their merriment fuelled with wine and, later on, brandy.

With the time being after eleven, the dining room was nearly empty. The general had fallen asleep at his table, his head bowed forward.

"I do not want to end up in here, old and decrepit, dining alone, pissed and asleep at my table," said the Englishman.

They all looked across the room towards the slumped figure of the general.

"I want my life to count for something," said the Indian.

"Well, my life is not going to bloody well count for God, I'll tell you that!" said the Englishman.

"Ya," said the South African, "but what a bloody mess the world is in."

"I have a friend in Washington," said the American, "and he says that this situation with

Russia and her friends is going to go on for at least ten, maybe twenty years, maybe longer. America will be at war with another country before long. There are plenty of senior people who are seriously paranoid about the spread of Communism."

"I'm not going to fight another bloody world war. I lost everyone in my family in the last one," said the Englishman.

"The thing I hate is the way we treat this planet," said the Indian, "nuclear bombs, toxic coal smoke, cars everywhere you go. Our atmosphere is a thing of purity and beauty and we are being so ignorant and irresponsible. The smog in London was so thick last week, I walked past a bus that was crawling along Piccadilly. I made it to the Ritz before it did!"

"The world is chasing after money," said the South African. "It's greed. People are never satisfied with what they have. We saw it at school. I see it among my family and our friends."

"The world is deceived with ornament," said the Englishman.

"The human race is on a path to self destruction," said the American, "we have seen it throughout history. The conflicts are no longer between two nations, now they involve many nations. And the weapons are getting more efficient at wiping out large numbers. We could blow the world to pieces, then it would be game over for everybody."

"The world is deeply divided," said the South African, "and I don't see how that will change. Even a country like South Africa is divided. Because of apartheid, we will have a reaction of violence, sooner or later. The oppressed will rise up. How can the government be so stupid? Most of the leaders of the world don't know their ass from a hole in the ground!"

There was a pause while they pondered.

A waiter came over to their table.

"Shall I pour some brandy, Your Grace?" he asked.

The Englishman nodded and thanked him.

They stared into their glasses. The brandy glowed in the candlelight.

"I say, chaps, perhaps we should form a group," said the Englishman.

"A group with a very specific aim," said the Indian.

"The aim will be to unify different races and nations," said the South African.

"To end warfare," said the American.

"To save the planet from irresponsible human exploitation," said the Indian.

"To bring order to the utter chaos," said the Englishman.

There was another pause as they looked at each other.

"We will need to recruit new people very carefully," said the Indian.

"Yeah," said the American, "this might actually be the beginning of something."

"Let's meet here in twelve months time," said the Englishman, "when we have all finished university and we have had time to think upon it. If we decide to take it forward, we will have had time to consider how to proceed."

He stood and held out his glass of brandy.

The others followed suit.

"To the future of this world," said the Indian.

"To the future of our world," said the Englishman.

"While the rest of the world is planning the year ahead," said the South African, "we will plan the future."

* * * * * *

DAY 2

G1L3E290718RN052CBS4UBWM4C half opened his eyes, only for a moment.

Morning light leaked into the dormitory from the shaded windows, yet the young men around him were still asleep.

Could he have a name, he wondered. Mark.

Since he was a baby, he had only had a number.

He searched his memories to the time when he was a child at the Nursery. One of his earliest memories was waking up with the nurse's smiling face looking down at him. He must have been nearly four yours old. Those were sunny days. He and the other boys had laughed and played together.

When he was five, he was transferred to the school complex and the training had begun. There had been no laughter and no play. He was part of a unit of one hundred boys from that time on. They never saw the nurses again. The Supervisors instructed them in all their activities. They learnt English, Maths, IT and Science. They had daily fitness training. There was no team sport or anything competitive. In later years, there were additional courses in practical work like catering, laundry, cleaning, construction, gardening, woodwork, metalwork, textile work, industrial work and mechanics. Everything they did at school was preparation for their adult life as Workers. They were taught to suppress any independent thinking. There were no individual or competitive activities: no art or creativity, no learning music, except the Anthem of the New Order.

Every hour of every day was regimented. The Supervisors explained that they were learning to work for the Common Good, for the purpose of Unity, for 100 per cent Carbon Neutrality, and for the harmony of the world. All religion had been purged in the War of Unification. They were taught about the excesses of the old era, and how the planet had been on the verge of irreversible damage and catastrophe. They were shown how many of the natural habitats in the world had recovered. They were taught that the purpose of their young lives was to serve and obey the Executive. They learnt that the Executive were the enlightened leaders of Global Unification.

They learnt placid acceptance of their roles. Whatever they were instructed to do, they should do without questioning. Questions were against the Golden Rule of serving the Common Good. Through learning acceptance of the New Order, they were steered away from independent thought. If a child asked a question, they would ask the group if the question was for the Common Good and if it accepted the New Order. What was enforced was that the individual should be the servant of the group. Their identity was the unit, and the unit was part of the whole number of units of Workers: a vast army. If they refused to participate, they were removed. They were not told what happened to anyone who was removed.

From the age of eleven, they learnt how to observe other units of children in other zones. Giving an alert tag on another child was keeping the Golden Rule. They were taught that flagging up a child meant that he could be helped by his teachers. The child could receive more schooling in the ways of the New Order and be prepared so that they would be able to contribute as an adult.

There were no religious festivals. At the onset of the New Order, Christmas had been eradicated along with all other events in the calendar that had any history or any association with a religion. His generation of Level Three Workers had never known any of these. The year was marked by the changing of the seasons in the city. There was a week every year to mark the time when the New Order was launched. The calendar was counted from the start of the New Order.

The notes for Rise sounded and the room came alive. Mark followed the routine. He dressed and went to breakfast. When he went to place his hand over the scanner screen, the voice spoke his identity number and said,

"Today you will work in Observation Room 412 until lunch, then you will work in Loading Bay 048 until dinner."

* * * * * *

In the heart of London, the immaculate figure of President Hussain was taking his seat on the throne on the raised area in the Operations

Room in the glazed courtyard of Buckingham Palace. He gestured for the staff to sit.

"What have you got?"

He addressed the elegant woman sitting at the desk to his right. His manner was as someone who expects his every command to be obeyed instantly.

"Good morning President, we have identified and located the Level Three Potential Rebel, code Charlie Thirty-Five Sixty-Four, in Sector Four in New Birmingham. May we proceed with the interception?"

The President looked at some of the screens showing the target. There was a call sound on another screen next to the president - a girl's face came up.

President Hussain raised a finger and touched the glass on his desk.

"Hello my Poppet, hold on a moment for grandpa."

He touched the screen again.

"Take him down now," he said to the woman, "then extract information."

He moved his attention back to the girl, his hand touching the glass again.

"What are you up today, my Pudding?"

"We're going on a trip to visit Hadrian's Wall today!" replied the girl.

* * * * * *

In Sector Four in New Birmingham, Mark was taking the same route as the day before. He passed Workers walking to their different sections.

Suddenly he noticed there was a man in Level Three Worker clothes running flat out towards him.

The man was within ten metres of him when two figures in black dived at the runner and all three skidded across the floor to Mark's left.

The three figures convulsed on the ground as the two men in black struggled to restrain the runner. The runner was trying to shout something but one man in black punched him in the face. Then the man was kneeling on the runner's chest and holding him down. The other man in black taped his mouth and jammed a needle in the runner's neck, squeezing the syringe, and then he thrust a black hood over his head. The Worker was dragged away, hands taped and body limp.

The passing Workers seemed to barely notice. Mark continued to Room 412.

The Supervisors surrounded him.

"Have you anything to report?" asked the senior one, a finger raised.

Mark shook his head.

The Supervisor pointed to a desk and their eyes all followed his movement across the room.

Mark worked on observation as before, but today his mind was active, wondering why the man had been intercepted and what had happened to him.

* * * * * *

At the remains of a Roman fort on Hadrian's Wall in Northern England, a drone transporter touched down and a group of sixteen school children and two teachers spilled out. They explored the ruins of the ancient walls.

A teacher called the children together and asked one of them to touch a button on a screen she was holding. A three dimensional hologram sprung up over the walls to show the extent of the original fort. The children murmured their approval. Voices explained the purpose of the wall, how the Romans had used the site and how the fort had linked with others along the line of fortification. The teacher sent the children to wander through the rooms.

While this was happening, a sniper, camouflaged to blend with the hillside, was training his weapon on the group. He followed one little girl in his sights. The display identified her as the target. He zoomed in on her head as she stood, looking at a display. He pulled the trigger. A ball of granite, the size of a grape, shot out at high velocity and struck the girl on her forehead. She fell to the floor, her body motionless. Two classmates went over to her. One screamed. The two teachers ran over to the girl's body. One teacher knelt, pulled on gloves from a medical bag and checked her pulse.

"I'll call the emergency services. You get the children away from here," said the teacher who was kneeling.

The second teacher stood staring.

"Contact school," continued the first teacher. "Get someone to meet you at the next stop. They can cover me. I'll go to the hospital. You go. Now."

The force of that last word jolted the second teacher into action.

As the second teacher turned to herd the children towards the drone transporter, the first teacher touched her screen.

"We need an air ambulance immediately, code red," she said.

"We have your location and details. How many casualties?" came the response.

"One nine year old female. She collapsed suddenly, without warning."

"Air ambulance alerted. Time to arrival: six minutes, fifty seconds. Can you send us images?"

"Affirmative. Top priority. The casualty is the granddaughter of President Hussain," said the teacher.

The teacher pressed pause on the screen. She looked around her but she was alone. She adjusted the body and smudged the forehead of the girl with dirt around where a stone protruded. She found the ball of granite and slipped it into her pocket. Then she took some video footage of the girl's position on the ground.

The drone transporter with the school group took off and headed South.

* * * * * *

Some time after morning tea break, Mark asked a Supervisor for a loo break. The Supervisor gave a small nod and he left the room.

The WC was along the corridor.

He was washing his hands when he was aware of a man standing at another basin next to him. They were alone in the room.

He glanced at the man in the mirror.

With a jolt, Mark realised that he had seen him before: it was the man in his dream!

"Mark," said the man, looking straight ahead into the mirror, his mouth hardly moving,

"My name is Sebastian. If you want to learn who you are, give me a sign by washing your face."

Mark's mouth fell open a fraction.

His eyes stared into the mirror for a moment.

His eyebrows furrowed slightly.

Mark bent and scooped water onto his face.

The man continued, "You are going to be moved so that we can have a chance to talk. I will see you later. Carry on as normal. Be careful, they are watching you."

The man turned to leave. As he passed behind him, he brushed against Mark's arm. The movement was enough to jab a small needle into Mark's arm and deliver a dose of antidote.

Mark dried his hands and face then walked back to his station in Room 412. His stride was the same as before but his eyes were more active, like they were taking in new surroundings.

Inside Room 412, he slipped back to his place. The Supervisors were looking his way. He kept his focus on the screen and worked in his usual manner until the notes that signaled the end of the session.

He made his way to the canteen.

He passed the place where the runner had been taken. The floor was clean and there was no sign of a struggle.

He ate lunch in his usual place, while the music and Announcements played. The faces and numbers of Workers who were to be awarded a Spring Holiday Break were shown.

When it was his turn at one of the information scanner screens, he placed his hand on the screen. "You will report to Sick Bay 734 in the Hospital Complex immediately," said the voice.

He tried again, just to make sure. The voice repeated the same instruction.

The Sick Bay block was some distance away, in the Hospital Complex. His steps were the normal, unhurried stride of any Worker in his unit. Silently, he counted his steps.

At last, he reached the Sick Bay section and took a lift to Level 7. The corridor was spotless, empty and smelt of antiseptic. He came to a white door marked 734 and paused. He took a deep breath, knocked and opened the door. A male nurse looked up and got up from behind a desk. He wore a white mask over his face. Beyond, there was a corridor with doors on either side where there must be a number of wards.

The nurse came over to him. He held a scanner that he waved in front of his chest, his eyes and his face, and then scanned his hand.

"Viral infection 623" said the electronic voice.

The nurse calmly led him along the corridor to a ward and showed him his bed, then the lockers and washing area. Following the nurse's instruction, he took off his boots and his day gear, showered and changed into the hospital long shirt, pyjamas and slippers and climbed into the bed. The smell reminded him of his childhood in the Nursery. Some of the tension in his muscles eased. Gentle sounds were played in the ward.

A doctor wearing a mask came to check him over. He held a sleek, black scanner and moved it over his whole body.

"Some facial acne; eczema on hands and legs; verrucas on left foot," the doctor reeled off a list of ailments to the nurse, who stood beside a trolley with an array of instruments. The nurse passed him a tool that looked like a torch, not much bigger than a pen. The doctor went methodically around the areas of eczema and zapped every area with a flash of bright light. He used a similar instrument on the acne. He took another tool and set about treating the verrucas. When he was done, he grunted and nodded. He instructed the nurse to maintain the medication and then left.

The nurse brought him water and two small white pills with minute numbers.

"You need to rest," he said, and went about his business in the ward.

Mark surveyed the room. There were two lines of beds and windows on the end wall. Most of the beds were empty but there were two other male patients in the beds near him. The screens showed a film about butterflies and their habitats.

Later on the nurse brought him supper on a tray and more medication. The food was similar to what he was used to in the canteen. He ate it all then settled down to rest. He soon fell asleep.

He had a dream: he was being carried along in a trench of fast moving water. The water was dark grey. Pieces of dirt were raining down on the conduit so the water was getting increasingly darkened. He struggled to push away the filth but his efforts were in vain.

* * * * * *

President Hussain was standing in his dressing room with two butlers and two aides. The screen on the wall connected with his daughter-in-law. She was at the hospital.

"How is she?" he asked.

"It's not looking good," the woman said. "The doctors say she is in a coma. She is stable but they cannot say how long it will be before she comes around. They are running more tests."

"How are you doing?" asked the President.

The woman did not answer. Her eyes welled and she dabbed her nose with a tissue.

"Don't worry. We will get the best doctors onto it. I have a formal dinner tonight but I will call you later."

The screen went blank.

The President turned to his aides.

"What does the report say about the cause?" he asked.

"The teachers said she fell without warning," replied one aide. "Her only injury was the impact to her head."

"I want this thoroughly investigated. I want people crawling all over that site first thing in the morning. This might be a plain accident. Or it might be foul play. Find the teachers. Debrief them fully. If that turd Sandher is behind this, he will get what is coming to him. With interest."

* * * * * *

Mark awoke because a hand was shaking his arm. He looked up and found the nurse was standing with Sebastian next to him.

Mark stared at them.

"It's decision time. This is very important. If you want to come to our meeting, it's time to get dressed," said Sebastian. "If, on the other hand, you want to go back to the unit and carry on just as you were, we can arrange that right away - you'll forget all about us, about coming here. If you come to the meeting with me, you will begin to find out who you are. It's time to decide because there is no going back if you come with us now."

"Join you," said Mark.

"Are you sure?" asked Sebastian, studying his face.

"Yes," replied Mark.

Mark dressed.

The other two young men in the ward were also getting ready.

They stood together and Sebastian addressed the three of them.

"There is a Supervisor who patrols the corridors some nights. We'll have to hide if he is on the prowl. He's called Hansford. His face looks like a weasel and he's just as unpleasant. If he catches someone, he reports Hansford catches him immediately. Do exactly as we say, and you'll be fine."

The nurse, Michael, led the four of them out of the ward, to a door. He checked the corridor and led them to some back stairs. They moved quietly. At the bottom of the stairs they headed along several more corridors. There were places where they waited while the nurse went to check that the coast was clear.

Uncertainty hung over Mark like a circling vulture: was he safe? Could he trust these people? Was it a trap? Would he be taken away with a hood over his head like the runner he saw?

Michael motioned to them to listen.

They could make out the sound of footsteps.

Michael beckoned them into a store and closed the door.

The sound of the footsteps was amplified in the bare corridor. They passed the door and continued.

They waited in silence.

The sound of footsteps faded.

They emerged into the corridor and continued on their way.

Eventually they reached a metal door. Michael listened intently then, when he was sure it was safe, he ushered them through and closed the door behind them.

It was as dark as a tomb inside but Sebastian and Michael had torches. They led the way down metal stairs and along a tunnel with many coloured pipes of various sizes. The temperature in the tunnel was uncomfortable: it was much warmer than the corridors.

At last they came to a door in a recess to one side of the tunnel. Sebastian opened it and they went into a dimly lit chamber. It was cool in here. Sebastian opened the first of three large, solid doors, closing each one carefully behind them before opening the next.

They entered a room with a high vaulted ceiling. There were about thirty men standing in a huddle. They turned as they approached.

An older man stepped forward and greeted Sebastian and Michael with a hug, then faced the three of them.

"Hello, my name is John Richardson. We are part of the church. We come here in secret to meet, to pray, to share and to worship. You will learn what I mean by these. You are here because you have been called in some way. There will be plenty of time to talk. We will meet here every night unless we are directed otherwise. There will be lots of time to answer your questions."

Mark could not remember when he had last asked anyone a question.

"You three, Mark, Johnson and Sanjay, you were all approached yesterday morning by Sebastian. The Lord showed you to us some time back, and we have been praying for you constantly since. Two nights ago, he made it clear that it was time for Sebastian to speak with you because you were ready. He showed us when, where and how Sebastian should make contact with you. We welcome you to our group."

The men in the group came forward and some shook their hands. This was a strange gesture to Mark.

John continued,

"We pray to God to add to our number. God gave us visions of the three of you. We have helped many young men like you. We want to help you begin to learn who you are and who God is. We know that this is a strange experience for you but it's the beginning of an amazing adventure. You may not have any questions yet. You will find that as you learn more, your mind will be more and more activated. You will have time in the Sick Bay to read and think and pray and rest. And just be. Every night, we would like you to join us here. Sebastian will bring you. We are here to serve you and help you. We would like to pray for you. We want to talk to God about you. Is that okay?"

All three nodded.

For Mark, this seemed like it could be another dream. For years, he had only known the cold instructions of Supervisors, the reports of the Announcers and what he had seen on the screens. The care this older man had for each of them was apparent, and it had a calming effect on his worries.

"Okay, close your eyes and we will place our hands on you and we will ask God to do some good things for you."

Men gathered around each of the three of them and began muttering words Mark could not understand. He heard John's voice.

"Father, we bless you and thank you for three more of your children. You have drawn them out of the darkness and into the light. We ask you now to touch them by the Spirit. Lord, let them feel your presence here with us now and in the coming days…"

Mark's eyes were closed. To begin with he felt nothing, but then he sensed a warm glow as he stood with five men around him. Their hands were on his shoulders, arms and back.

"God, touch their hearts. Give them eyes to see and ears to hear. We ask you to begin the healing tonight. We release the goodness of God over them."

Then John began to sing with strange words. The men of the group joined in. The sound they made was like nothing he had heard before. He felt like he was lifting and floating up into blue brightness. Some words came into his mind.

"*I have been waiting for you.* "

He felt safe like when he had been a small child in the Nursery. He had not felt love since that time, and he could not put into words what he was now feeling. It was like coming home after a very long and lonely journey.

"Let's worship together," said John, "D, Steve and Jake, will you lead us?" The three men he addressed moved forward. Two picked up strange objects while the other stood at a long thin box on a stand. Music filled the room as they played. The other men gathered round and sang together now in English. It was a song that spoke of the goodness of God. Mark stared with large eyes. He had heard music every day in the unit, but he had never seen it played. The words of the song were projected from the box on the stand. Mark could follow the words from the 3D hologram that was projected in the space above their heads.

The men were moving onto another song and some were lifting up their arms. They seemed to be the best of friends. Mark struggled to accept that it really happening and was not a dream. He stood in the same spot, wanting to move closer.

Now they were clapping to a new song. The words and the music washed over Mark like waves. The vibrations seemed to make his whole body resonate. He felt like he wanted to join in, but had no idea how. There was a disconnection that prevented him.

Now the men were kneeling, some were lying on their stomachs, arms out. The music quietened down to silence.

After a bit, John prayed, "Thank you God for the freedom you give, thank you for the healing you bring. Bless us and keep us safe until we meet again. Holy Spirit guide us in everything. In your name, we pray…"

"Amen," the men all said together: it was a word of agreement.

They were offered some refreshments and the three nodded their thanks, still awkward.

Sebastian and Michael led them back to the tunnel and along to the metal door. The journey back to the Sick Bay seemed to Mark to not take long. His mind was full of the experiences of the meeting.

They arrived back in the ward. Sebastian said he would come for them the next night, and he said his goodbyes. They washed, changed and climbed into their beds.

Mark felt lighter that night and he was soon asleep.

In a dream, he was surrounded by darkness. In the distance, there was a glow that penetrated the gloom. He went nearer and realised that it was a door. He put his hand on the handle. He deliberated, hesitating. If he opened the door, there would be no going back.

* * * * * *

The hospital where the President's granddaughter lay was all quiet in the dead of night. A nurse on night duty approached her room, passing the security guards. The nurse checked her pulse and consulted her charts. The security guards lost interest and looked towards a large screen showing a game. No one saw the nurse add a dose to the drip solution that fed into her arm.

* * * * * *

Flashback Saturday 16th January 1954

It was another cold night in London.

The four friends met over dinner in a private room in the Royal Motoring Club in Pall Mall.

The walls were hung with paintings and photographs of racing cars.

The table was littered with the remnants of their meal.

A waiter poured out the brandy and then slipped out of the room.

"So, come on chaps, what do we think?" asked the American, seeing that they were alone. "Do we go quietly into the night, merging with the mass of humanity, or are we going to aspire to do something about this wayward world, as we talked about a year ago?"

"I am certainly convinced we should initiate something," said the Indian prince.

"We could all live very well on our wealth," said the English duke. "We could marry well, play well, and leave our fortunes to our offspring but be remembered for little when we are dead and gone. I say, let's contrive a bright future. Let's lay our hand on the world and see if we can guide its destiny."

The others nodded.

"I think we need to infiltrate different areas," said the American. "We need to gather intelligence so I have been thinking about how to use my contacts in New York, Washington and in the CIA. I am going to join the family bank in New York. It's expected of me. I can use my position there. I will learn a huge amount about who really wields the power. Money follows power. They go together."

"Like bat and ball," said the Englishman.

"I want to find out who is doing what," said the South African. "I have been thinking about media and journalism, so I think I am going to join an international press agency for a while. I want to travel and find out what is happening in different countries. It should give me lots of contacts. I might find others who will join us."

"What about your minor mining interests?" asked the American.

"Well," the South African grinned, "they are finding diamonds. I may have to divide my time somewhat. But I will not be going hungry."

The others laughed.

"What about you, Uday?"

The American had turned to the Indian.

"Science is my passion, as you know," said the Indian, "so I want to explore how the scientific community could serve our cause. I have been thinking about what science could do in a world under central control. I believe that science could be essential to what we aim to achieve."

"The more I think about the world's problems, the more I think the only possible solution will have to be a single government over every nation," said the South African. "We cannot have a few rogue nations doing their own thing, they would be like rotten apples in the barrel. They would affect all the other apples until the whole barrel was rotten and we would be back to where we started."

"I think you are right, old chap," said the Englishman. "That all sounds very promising. As for me, I have to keep an eye on the estates of course, but I am interested in how Western Europe is going to develop. Can they work together to achieve some form of unity? I fancy a spot of travel: Berlin, Paris and Rome for starters. A bit of rubbing shoulders with the great and the good."

"Well, you are rather good at that, old bean," said the American.

"We will need to consider the criteria for recruiting more members to our esteemed group," said the Indian. "The criteria will include the trust, discretion and secrecy we will require."

"And genuine commitment to the cause," said the American.

"And motivation, and shared passion," said the South African.

"And a level of wealth," said the Englishman. "Influence is going to be essential."

"I think we are going to need lots of scientists," said the Indian. "Although many of them may not have access to substantial funds."

"We will want people who are not content with the existing structures and who yearn for greater power," said the South African.

"Power is very seductive to most people," said the American.

"In our different spheres, let us compile a list of potential members of our group," said the Indian.

"And let's also have a black list of people who will never join us, who will oppose us whatever happens," said the Englishman. "We will have to consider what we do with them, so that they do not hinder us and our aims can be achieved."

"There will be a middle group of people who we will be able to turn to our side, given the right circumstances," said the American. "Maybe a nudge, maybe a push."

"I do not know how we will do it but I am fully committed," said the South African.

They stood to drink a toast.

"To the future the world does not yet know," said the South African.

"And we happy few," said the Englishman.

* * * * * *

DAY 3

The room in the hospital where the President's granddaughter was being treated had come to life. The girl had woken, as from a deep sleep. She was weak but was able to speak softly to her delighted mother. Her doctors were confident she would make a full recovery.

* * * * * *

Mark woke late in the morning and took a few moments to work out where he was. Then he remembered the Sick Bay, the doctor's visit, meeting Sebastian, the journey to the meeting. The meeting. He closed his eyes again. He remembered the warm glow in his chest; the sense of floating up into the sky; the men's voices rising in song; the friendship the men had together.

The nurse came over with a tray of breakfast and hot tea, and two more white pills. He was hungry. He sat up and worked his way through cooked eggs, potato, mushrooms and tomato, then toast and jam.

The nurse returned and said,

"My name is Michael. You can rest and sleep and read. The ward is yours. If you want anything, just press this."

He showed him a button on a small controller.

Mark leant back with a sigh. In the unit, every single day was dictated by the instructions from the information screens. The notes were the regular signals, directing the whole unit. Here, he could browse on the hand-held device, read the magazines or a book from the shelves in the ward. He could shower when he wanted. He felt a sense of liberty that he had not had since his days in the Nursery, as a young child. The two other men were in a similar predicament. They were not used to a little freedom. They glanced at each other but did not speak. They all drifted into a sleep. The nurse woke them at lunchtime. They ate and slept again. While they slept, the nurse checked on them regularly.

* * * * * *

President Hussain was sitting at a desk in a drawing room in Buckingham Palace when the two aides were shown in.

He looked up from the report he was reading.

"Gentlemen, what have you found out regarding my granddaughter's accident?"

"Well, Sir, there is nothing concrete we can point to as suspicious. It's a mystery why she fell and suffered the head trauma. We interviewed the teachers and the children. There was no weapon found. She woke up this morning without any recollection of the incident. We understand that she was standing still when she collapsed, so she did not trip."

"Do you suspect foul play?" asked the President. His expression was penetrating.

The two aides looked at each other.

"We are not sure, Sir," replied the senior aide. "The thing that does not add up is that the doctors said that it was unusual for a fall to induce a coma. She was well and healthy on the morning of the visit."

The President pinched his lower lip.

"My hunch is that this was a hit. I have an ugly feeling that it was Sandher. I want you to look at his family; watch their movements.

Give me some options on a hit on one of his grandchildren. Not fatal. Be discrete."

* * * * * *

Later, they ate supper and Mark had a growing anticipation for the hour when Sebastian would come for them. The two other men seemed to be similarly watching the clock.

He lay down and explored his memories. There were times in the Nursery when he was allowed to play with the other boys. They sometimes played a catching game. There was a sandpit where they loved to make roads and dig tunnels and drive their trucks. There was a tree in their playground and sometimes he used to feel content, sitting under its branches. Near the base of the trunk, there were two lumpy growths where he could perch. It was a place of stillness to him: a place to linger and be. He used to feel that that he was not alone. There was a sense of being protected.

At last, he spotted Sebastian with Michael. They came over and asked the three to get ready. It did not take them long to dress.

Soon they were retracing their steps down back stairs to the long empty corridors. Mark recognised the places where Michael would stop and check for Hansford. It felt like a game of cat and mouse: his heart beat in his chest with a mixture of excitement and anxiety.

They made it to the safety of the tunnel. When they came to the last of the three solid doors, Mark felt his heart lift a little in his chest. He was glad to be back.

The men greeted them. There were more men than the previous night. John came forward,

"Are you ready to meet with the Lord?" he asked them.

They nodded shyly.

"Let's begin with waiting on the Lord for his direction."

They gathered into a circle and John opened in a prayer, then they all fell silent, some standing, and some kneeling.

After some time, John prayed,

"Lord, come and speak to us, give us words and pictures. Spirit, guide us. We ask you to give us ears to hear and eyes to see."

Mark's eyes were closed. He heard different voices as different men spoke.

"I get a sense that the Lord wants to remind us that he will protect us - never will he leave us or abandon us."

"I get the words - "Come close to me, and I will come close to you.""

"I see a picture of the Lord touching Johnson, Sanjay and Mark. He is healing their hearts. Their hearts were like stone but they now beat with life."

"I sense that he wants to give the three of them a close friendship. They are like brothers."

Then John said, "let's wait on the Lord for these three."

He asked for wisdom and invited the Lord to speak.

"I sense the Lord saying that Sanjay is gifted in teaching."

"I see them playing music together. Others are gathering round to join them. They feel the joy of true worship."

"The Lord wants you to know that he has known you from the moment you were conceived in your mother's body. He knows all about you and everything you have been through."

"Do you remember that song Jasper taught us? The one that goes, 'He is God.' I feel like we should sing it over them."

This last voice sounded like Sebastian.

There was some movement, and then the musicians began to play a song.

It had a gentle opening, and then they sang, "Who is there that loves me as I am?"

As Mark listened to the words about a loving father who wipes tears away, who gives strength to face the day, he felt something rising in his chest. Before he knew it, he felt a strange sensation in his closed eyes. His face was tingling and eyes were welling. Two little tears crept out from his lids and slid down his cheeks. He sank to his knees then dropped his face onto the floor. He wanted to bow down to this God. He felt that He was going to do the things he had heard them pray: he was going to restore him to the man who he was supposed to be. The thought had a sense of certainty. More tears rolled down onto the floor.

A voice said, "let's all pray for Mark."

His eyes were shut but he sensed bodies moving close to him and hands placed on him. Someone asked for the Lord to show him what he wanted to do.

"Lord, give him eyes to see and ears to hear what you are doing now."

"What do you see or feel, Mark?" one of them asked.

Mark spoke slowly, "I see a bridge. It crosses a deep valley, with cliffs on either side. A man dressed in white is standing on the bridge. He is reaching his arms out to me."

Some different voices then prayed for revelation for him, for God's love to draw him, for peace to fill his heart.

"What do you see or feel now?"

"The man is taking my hand and leading me over. It is beautiful on the other side, like a garden."

"Mark," said one of them, "do you want to be sealed as a child of God?"

"Yes. Definitely." Mark had never been more sure of anything.

"Jesus is God's son. He came to earth a long time ago. He died as a sacrifice to make a way for us to come back to God. His death paid the price of our wrong. When we were enemies of God, he made peace through his death. When you receive him as Saviour and Lord, you cross over from death to life. "

The man led him for the next prayer and Mark repeated after him, in his heart.

"Lord, I come to you. Take me as I am. I ask you to forgive me for not living for you. From today, I belong to you. My life is yours."

Mark felt weak, like he was surrendering. Then something strange happened. It was like a dam in his heart had been broken and a flood was released. Tears filled his eyes. He did not feel sad; it was more relief. He felt that at last he knew that God was there and that if he died tonight, he had at last lived. Nothing mattered more. His cheeks were marked from the steady stream of tears. He let them flow.

Most of the men were praying for Sanjay now, but three men still had hands on Mark. They were praying quietly, under their breath so that Mark could hardly hear what they said.

Johnson was prayed for after Sanjay.

The group agreed they were ready for some more worship.

"I believe in You," they sang. The song had a faster beat.

The next song had a drum beat that reminded Mark of pictures of marching soldiers, "Praises rising, our eyes are looking to you," it went.

The words seemed to speak directly to him.

"In your presence, all sins are washed away."

Mark felt his heart joining in the worship of a God who saves.

The men around him were singing with strength, passion and joy.

The third song was more intimate, and brought on tears in another wave. There was now a damp patch on the floor by his feet.

"I fall at your feet, and I worship you now, Jesus," went the song.

There was a mixture of feelings in Mark's heart. There was gladness, relief, yearning, things he could not name, and he just let it wash over him. He did not have to work it up. He let it flow, even when he did not understand what was truly happening. It was like falling into the strong current of a river and being taken downstream. He felt that this was the most important moment of his life. He knew that he would never forget this night.

Much later, they said their farewells. Some of the men gave them hugs. One of the brothers held Mark. Mark's whole body relaxed in the embrace. He felt that he belonged in this motley group of men. He looked back at the group as they made their way to the first of the heavy doors. Sebastian led them quietly back to the Sick Bay. They whispered good night and washed before falling gratefully into bed.

In a dream that night, Mark found himself wandering dimly lit passageways. He had the feeling he was underground. As he wandered, he came across other people. It was like a party except no one wanted to talk to him; everyone was hostile and aggressive. They told him to go away. Everyone was fearful of everyone else. Everyone wanted to be alone and yet they were isolated and horribly unhappy. He was lost and could not find the way out of this strange subterranean place.

* * * * * *

Flashback Saturday 15th January 1955

The four friends met in the Swiss Alps on the invitation of the Englishman.

After a day's skiing, they were back at their hotel and were taking a sauna.

"What on earth are we doing in Davos, Switzerland?" asked the Indian.

"A change of scenery, old chap," said the Englishman. "Frightfully good for the constitution. Actually, I think I am going to buy a chalet here. I think this skiing caper is jolly good fun and it attracts the types with wealth and influence that we are after."

"What he really means is that there are plenty of pretty girls who flock here," said the American. "I expect a tall, handsome, titled, wealthy Englishman gets plenty of interest."

"Well, there are a few opportunities for behaving badly," replied the Englishman, "but consider: the Swiss have a reputation as trusted bankers of discretion. They draw the world's rich. The rich like to play. And where do they play in winter? Places like this. Travel is getting easier and cheaper. Skiing is going to rise in popularity, I am sure of it."

"I expect next you will be telling us we should buy land here," said the South African.

"I do fancy buying up some land in the valley, yes indeed," replied the Englishman. "There are a couple of farms I have my eye on. But I have been thinking. Being rich is like being a member of an exclusive club. Like school. This is a venue for that club. The rich come here like bees to honey."

"You are probably right, old chum," said the American. "And besides, you would not miss the summer season in England or the shooting season in Scotland! Do tell us: what have you learnt about the possibility of unity in Europe?"

"Well, there are signs that France, Germany, Italy and The Netherlands want to sit at a table with a number of others," replied the Englishman. "They want to have some kind of cast iron guarantee that another war in Europe will never happen again. They see a long-term agreement as their best option. They think that forming an economic group will be beneficial. The Treaty of Paris was the first step."

"Do you think they will be able to achieve economic union?" asked the South African.

"Frankly, I think they will be able to put something in place," replied the Englishman, "but I would bet that it will not be permanent, despite their best efforts. There is deep distrust and there are significant differences that I think will never be resolved. Take the Swiss. They are profoundly independent. The lesson of the last forty years for them is simple: do not join in the shambles of European politics and power struggles. They will not be a part of it."

"What have you learnt in the United States?" asked the Indian.

"The impasse between the US and the USSR is going to be with us for many years," replied the American. "The propaganda is heavy on both sides and the gulf is wide - as wide as the ocean. I hate to say it but I think our aims cannot be achieved while there are fingers hovering over the red buttons on both sides, and while the threat of nuclear war is so imminent. Khrushchev is an old school Soviet and

Eisenhower is a product of the land of the free. They are poles apart. I think it is going to take years for a new generation to move into power and for there to be any warming of relations."

"Then this may the winter of our discontent," said the Englishman, "so I say let us eat, drink and be merry while we wait for our opportunity. Come on, one and all."

He opened the outside door and threw himself naked into the deep snow.

"What?" cried the Indian, "I risked my life on the slopes today and now you want to die of exposure?"

He hopped from foot to foot while the other three lay laughing in the snow.

Back in the sauna, the Indian cleared his throat and said, "Gentlemen, I have my eye on my first recruit."

The others turned their attention towards him.

"She is a young post-graduate in London. Biochemistry is her field. I went to hear her lecture on how drugs affect the brain. She held the audience in an iron fist. Very controlling, very intelligent. A prime candidate to join us, I believe."

"Come, come, old fruit," said the Englishman, "do you think a woman will think as we do?"

"Indeed. In time, you will eat your hat," said the Indian with a smile. "I have been pondering what we said about a central government. I have been thinking about how bees are organised. All the Worker bees serve the queen bee. They do not question their role. An interesting model, I suggest."

The American studied his face then turned to the Englishman.

"So what has His Grace got planned for our entertainment tonight?"

"Dinner in a restaurant that serves a rather delicious local dish," replied the Englishman, "washed down with copious quantities of local beer, then we shall sally forth and go dancing. The stakes are as follows: two pounds if you get intimate with a French or Italian gal, three pounds for a German or a Swiss."

"And ten pounds if she's a lesbian!" added the American.

The laughter could be heard along the corridor.

DAY 4

President Hussain was having breakfast in a private dining room. The two aides stood while he was flicking through pages on a screen.

"This one. The man in the race. How sure are you that you can execute successfully?" he asked, without looking up.

"We are one hundred per cent, Sir."

"Okay. Do it. But he must not die."

* * * * * *

They slept well into the morning. The nurse, Michael, brought Mark breakfast when he roused. He wheeled up a table and chairs so that the Johnson and Sanjay could sit with them. Michael asked them how the meeting had gone. He sat down while they took it in turns to relate how they had been prayed for.

"It felt like a turning point for me," said Sanjay. "I feel like my life up to now has been like stumbling around in a thick fog, and now the fog is clearing and I can see the sunshine. I can see where I am. People were dark shapes in the fog, but now I am starting to see more clearly."

"I think I felt like I belonged in my unit, but it was cold and unfriendly," said Johnson, "and now I am really glad to be part of this group. I want to go every night. I have no idea what is going to happen to me, but I am not going to worry about that. I want to follow the Lord. I want to know so much more. This is a completely new thing for me. I feel like a young child inside."

Michael smiled at them. "That is such great news. I should tell you something. When you were back in your units, you would lie down to sleep at night and your whole unit would be treated with a gas called NIG312: Neural Interceptor Gas, Level 3, version 12. It was specially developed to keep Level Three Workers placid so that they would not feel emotions. This Sick Bay does not have outlets for gas because it interferes with healing from viruses and other sicknesses. It normally takes about three days for the effects of the gas to wear off. That is partly why you feel so different now. Before, it was difficult to interact meaningfully with other people. Now you will be more and more in touch with your feelings. It might be strange at first. Be patient with yourselves while you get used to it. It is a gift that you are here together. You have so much to share. Take your time. There is no hurry. You will have lots to ponder and lots of questions."

"That explains why everyone in the unit would be all out together when the lights were turned off," said Sanjay. "In my unit, I can't remember one time when anyone got up in the night."

The other two nodded.

Mark told them about his dream and described the bizarre situation of encountering aggressive people in dark corridors.

"Let me tell you what that sounds like," said Michael. "Hell. It's a place of fear and rejection. Where everyone hates everyone else. There is no love, no peace, no trust."

The three of them were quiet.

"That aside, I have a suggestion for you today," Michael said with a bright glint in his eyes. He picked up the hand-held device by Mark's bed, and waved it to activate it.

"Watch this."

He held it up in front of them and said clearly, "Jesus is Lord." The screen went dark for an instant then it lit up with patterns of colourful rainbows.

"The device is voice activated. It flips to a whole new set of settings. On here now, you will find a library of Christian music, you can read the Bible, call up different Scriptures; listen to teachings on a menu of subjects and much more. See what you can find on it. You each have one. It will help you more than I can say."

The three murmured their thanks.

"I will see you at lunchtime." Michael took their plates and left them.

For the rest of the morning, they used the devices. Mark had never had an opportunity to listen to music of his own choosing. Back in the unit, the music was played for them, as it was in all areas. He scrolled through the lists. There were whole genres he had never encountered before: Rock, Pop, Hip Hop, Chillout, Soul, Rhythm & Blues, Reggae, Folk, Dance and several others. He had a growing sense of wonder that there was such breadth in music: so much creativity reflected in so many tunes and melodies. When he found a track he liked, he added it to a playlist. The more he tried different songs, the more he enjoyed it. It was like sampling lots of delicious pieces of food: there were so many different tastes. Before long, he had several playlists under headings like 'Joyful,' 'Intimate,' and 'Loud.'

When Michael brought them lunch, they gathered again to discuss what they had found in their searches on the devices.

Sanjay had spent the time listening to teaching. He told them that there were menus of talks about lots of different subjects. Each talk had images which came up and sometimes animations, film footage or footage of the speaker.

"A good series for you all to listen to today would be the series on salvation," said Michael.

Mark told them about how he had been exploring music and what a wide range there was.

Johnson had been looking into what information there was about the church. He had learnt that before the War of Unification, there had been millions of Christians in most countries, who were all part of the church.

"People who were Christians could meet openly, every week. They used to have buildings of their own," he said.

"The church has a long history in Europe, added Michael. "The way that most countries were organised was based to a large extent on Christian principles. Music has been a major part of worship in churches for centuries. It will be good if you find out more about the church in the present time. We have so much to learn and you three can help each other by sharing."

They talked on after Michael went off with their lunch things. Their eagerness to learn more led them to agree that they would meet later on and share what new things they had found.

Mark looked up some teaching on salvation. He watched a team of men and women explaining about how the death of Jesus opened a way to renew a relationship with God that had been broken with the first man. They mentioned that a person crosses over from death to life when they accept Jesus as saviour and Lord. It reminded him of his picture of the chasm with the bridge. He wanted to ponder the teaching, so he went back to his music playlist and listened to a song that had the words, "Hallelujah, gracious Saviour, Christ has come to show us the way."

He marveled again at the creativity of the artists who wrote and played these songs. He lay back and closed his eyes. Over three days, his life had taken such a significant turn that he could not even contemplate going back to the numb existence in the unit.

Michael came and asked them to dress. He took them upstairs to another room. It was a gym. He introduced them to the instructor. Michael asked him to do some sparing with them.

"Take any frustration out in the ring," he told them.

They took it in turns to box with the instructor.

Johnson went first. He threw punches that the instructor either blocked or dodged. He received some sharp jabs to the head cover and his breast. He charged the instructor but the instructor jumped out of the way. Eventually he managed to land some punches. The instructor called time out and Johnson was glad to retire. He was sweating and moving ponderously.

Sanjay and Mark fared little better and ended up weary and panting.

Michael led them back to the ward and they showered and dressed.

* * * * * *

Twenty miles West of London, the annual M25 night race was almost ready to start. On the starting grid, there were forty cars lined up in the four lanes. The start was flood lit and drones with camera crews and support crews hovered above. Near the middle of the line up there was a bright yellow Lamborghini. One of the stickers on the car read 'SANDHER.' The driver was staring at a large screen above the start line. As the countdown started, he lifted a small container he was holding to his nose and snorted the white powder.

The countdown reached zero and, with a roar, the cars took off towards the North like an angry swarm, with the fleet of drones following over-head. The numbers on the Lamborghini dashboard display scrolled up to one hundred and moved up higher as the driver accelerated and worked through the gears. Suddenly the driver's vision was blurred as the chemicals in his bloodstream reached his brain. The car slewed from side to side as the driver struggled to stay conscious; the controls seemed to not respond. The car veered off course, leaving the road and careering up a steep embankment. At the top, the car left the ground and sailed over a wooden fence, plunging into the crop and sliding in the soft soil, coming to a stand still in the field on its side. The body of the driver lay slumped, unconscious, as two rescue drones dropped into field.

* * * * * *

That night, they followed Michael and Sebastian down to the church meeting. The journey was uneventful except for one point where they spent a few minutes listening for footsteps.

Arriving at the church, Mark, Johnson and Sanjay all felt comfortable. They greeted the men and found it easy to chat to the members of the group.

The meeting began with prayer and a time of listening to the Spirit to see what directions he might give.

Led by John, they were prompted to ask the three newcomers if they understood what had happened and whether they felt secure that they were now saved, that they were sealed as children of God.

Sanjay shared what he had learnt from the teaching on salvation he had watched. Johnson said that he truly felt a Christian and a part of Christ's church.

"What about you, Mark?" one of them asked.

"I feel that I have crossed over like in the picture I had last night. My old life has gone. I am a new person in my new faith." Mark replied confidently.

"Can I be baptised?" asked Sanjay, "I read somewhere Jesus said we should repent and be baptised."

"Yes, of course," said John, "Come over here."

He led them over to another space, like a large recess. He pressed a button and a section of the floor moved back to reveal a small pool with steps going down in two places.

John asked Sanjay what he understood about baptism. Sanjay explained that he had read a story about an Ethiopian who had met one of the apostles. They talked in his chariot. When they came past some water, the Ethiopian had asked to be baptised.

John gave him a towel and a white robe and showed him where to change behind a screen. John told them that in the time of Jesus, people were baptised to show a change of allegiance from one merchant group to another.

When Sanjay emerged in his robe, two men were already in the water. He made his way carefully down the steps. He stepped into the water. It came above his waist.

They said a few words, asking him if he was sure he wanted to be baptised and when he nodded, they helped him to go under the water so that his whole body was submerged. He came up beaming, raising both hands high. The men clapped and cheered.

Johnson and Mark both said they wanted to be baptised. Long after, Mark remembered the moment he went down under the water: everything went dark, sounds were muffled, bubbles pushed past his face, his body relaxed. Then he rose up and was back in the light, with the water streaming off him, and he could hear the applause and cheering.

Mark felt relieved: he was now marked; it was a sign of his commitment; there was no going back; he was in deep.

The men agreed that it would be good to have a worship time.

"Let's raise the roof!" one of them joked, "my spirit is bursting to give thanks."

"Let's start with 'Praises Rising,'" said Jake.

Mark remembered some of the tune from the night before, and was able to join in. It was the first time he had sung freely since his days in the Nursery as a small child. He felt tears of joy mixed with sadness for the years that he had not used this gift. The men were gathered around the three and they stamped their feet on the floor with the drumbeat.

The next song was about what a good day the day of salvation is. They sang about sins washed away. The men were jumping up and down and throwing their arms in the air. They joined arms in a large circle around the musicians in the centre and danced. There was a line where they shouted together, "You have saved me." The three players continued by improvising, and some of the men took it in turns to lead chorus lines that they repeated together. Mark joined in, feeling some freedom. He could not remember if he had danced before, but he followed the others as best he could. The more he gave himself, the more freedom he felt. Soon, he was jumping and stamping his feet.

They sang several more songs of celebration.

Mark asked D if they could play the slower song he had found, with the words, "Hallelujah, Praise The Saviour, Christ has come and shown us the way."

To his surprise, they knew it, and with a smile, Steve started playing the opening bars on the keyboard. The men all sang together in a circle. When they got to the line, "I don't stand alone," they put their arms on each other's shoulders. Another wave of emotion went through Mark. He felt so happy to be accepted into this group, he could feel the tears coming again.

The musicians played on and some of the men spoke out prayers of thanks. In his heart, Mark joined in with every prayer. These were his brothers. He felt that a bond had been forged that would last for the rest of his life.

They spent time at the end of the meeting with hot cups of tea, sitting and chatting together in a big circle.

Johnson asked if they were all in units or if they were in Sick Bay like them.

"I am a Supervisor," said John.

"So am I," said Steve, the keyboard player. Most of the others were in units. "We hear the Spirit calling us to stay with our units so that we are available for anything he calls us to do, like making contact with new people, like when Sebastian contacted you.

"How do you spend your days?" asked Sanjay.

They explained that they followed the instructions given on the information screens.

"The difference is that we are awake, we are alive. We are free to pray and listen to the Spirit. It is exciting. Every morning, we rise and wait for the Lord to direct us. If he says, pray, we pray. If he says, speak to that man, we do it," explained one of them.

"How do you leave the units to get to the meetings?" asked Mark.

"The Lord makes everything we do possible," said another, patiently. "He showed us a way to avoid the gas. We have these, we slip them into our noses." He showed him a clever little filter device that fitted into his nostrils. "Then we leave after the others are asleep. We all know back ways to get down here."

"Are we going to have to go back to our units?" Mark asked the question that part of him did not want to ask.

John answered, sensing his worry,

"That is simple: we wait for the prompting of the Spirit. We will enquire with you, when he leads us to. The Spirit knows the times and places of all things. He helps and guides us all, exactly as we need. Whatever the Lord asks you to do, he will provide the means and he will give you grace to do it. He has plans for you and they will help you."

Mark made a mental note to look up the word 'grace' in the morning. He was relieved and he felt sure that the Lord would prepare him for whatever was in store.

Sanjay echoed his thoughts, "I want to follow the Lord where he leads. Before, I had nothing and now I feel like I have so much."

The others smiled at him and agreed.

Another question came to Mark.

"Are we rebels?" he asked.

John grinned at him.

"In a sense, I suppose we are. We come here in secret; we are breaking the rules being here. But we do what we do out of love. Love for the Lord, love for each other and love for the rest who do not yet know."

"But are you planning to put an end to the New Order?" Mark enquired.

John raised his eyebrows.

"No. But we pray for it to end. We long for freedom for everyone."

Later on, they said their farewells and headed with Sebastian to the tunnel. The corridors were silent as they slipped back up to the ward.

That night, Mark was able to relax like never before.

As he drifted off to sleep, he prayed, "Lord, my life is in your hands. Thank you for bringing me here."

His dream that night took him to a place he did not recognise. There were people working on different tasks, yet there was a remarkable sense of unity and purpose. They were preparing for something. He stood in a hiding place and watched them moving, speaking in quiet voices. No one noticed him. Their faces were calm but full of intent. Among them, Johnson and Sanjay were part of the group.

* * * * * *

Flashback Saturday 20th January 1990

The four friends stood together in a large conference room in Davos, Switzerland. They were surrounded by a large group of elegantly dressed people from every continent. On the wall in front of them they were screens showing groups of people gathered in other countries.

"Ladies and gentlemen," began the American. "Today we celebrate a watershed. The Cold War has officially ended! The historians of the world will write their accounts and they will not credit us with success in bringing the Soviet Union to its senses, but we know the truth.

"Phase Three preparation work can now begin in earnest. We have teams who are mapping the world's resources. Other teams are drawing up proposals for the locations and functions of the megacities. We have design teams who are working on the blueprints for the layouts of the cities. Our biochemical teams are making good progress towards creating the right types of control drugs we will need. The next ten years will be crucial in moving closer to our goal. We need progress in computer technology to advance to a point where computer use is universal in all developed countries. Then the time will come for us to surprise the world with our..." he paused, "little takeover! Timing is everything, as we well know."

"Let us drink a toast," said the Englishman. "To Phase Two completed and our success in bringing the Soviet Union into line with our aims."

The gathering responded and the champagne glasses in their hands were lifted.

DAY 5

President Hussain was clearly enjoying his break-fast. The two aides waited while he watched footage of the driver on the start grid and the car crash that followed on his screen.

He chortled.

"Excellent work. That will put Sandher in his place. How much did be lose, betting in the race?" he asked.

"We believe, Sir, that he had placed ten million credits on his grandson coming in the top three."

The President almost chocked on his coffee.

"Fantastic! Serve him right. You have made my day. They will not be posing in that car for a while."

* * * * * *

At breakfast that morning, Mark shared his dream and asked the others if they had had vivid dreams since they left the unit.

"The Lord often speaks to me in my dreams," said Michael.

"Why do you think that is?" asked Sanjay.

"I asked him one time," replied Michael, "and the reply I got was that our minds are so easily occupied when we are awake. In a dream, he has easy access to show us things or speak to us. Sometimes it is far from what we expect. You will see in the Scriptures, there are many examples of people hearing from the Lord in dreams, in many different ways."

"It was a dream that started the journey for me to be here," said Mark.

The others looked at him, waiting for him to continue.

"I had a dream of a huge storm, when normally I never had dreams."

"One of the effects of the gas I told you about is that your senses are dulled and you have dreamless sleep, like you are sedated," replied Michael.

"Mark, what was the dream?" enquired Johnson, looking steadily at him.

He told them about the awesome sandstorm. He remembered it clearly. He described how he carried on that day as if nothing had happened. He related how he had had the same dream the following night, except this time there had been Sebastian speaking his name.

Michael was clearly moved, hearing him tell his story. He wiped his eyes, smiled and said,

'The Lord answers our prayers in wonderful ways."

"What about you, Johnson?" asked Mark.

"It was Sebastian. I kept seeing him and he would smile at me with his eyes. One day, we travelled up in a lift together and without turning to me, he said, "there is someone who cares for you who wants to meet you. He is God. If you want to meet him, show me by rubbing your nose."

That morning I had been sitting in breakfast and a question came to me: "*Who really knows you?*" The thought stayed with me all morning. I started to realise that I was alone; no one around me really knew me. I was still thinking about it when he asked me. So I rubbed my nose. Later, I was directed here by the on-screen instructions and the rest you know."

Mark grinned then he asked, "What about you, Sanjay?"

"It was Sebastian for me too. I would pass him from time to time. He would sometimes say things to me out of the blue that matched what I was thinking about. One time, I was working in the canteen kitchen and he was there. I was thinking about whether I could tell if what I was doing was real, and not my imagination. He looked at me and he whispered, "The source of all truth is God."

"I just looked at him. We carried on as normal but it had an impact. I could not stop thinking about it."

"The next morning, we were there again and he said, "You can meet God. If you want to know what I am talking about, stop sweeping and tie your apron tighter." So I did. That same day, I came here. I was instructed by the screen like you two."

They looked at Michael.

"How did the information screen know to send us here?" asked Mark.

Michael smiled at them.

"We have people in all sorts of places. We have found ways to infiltrate the system. We sent a message and they arranged the instructions. It was easy. Now, excuse me, I have a few things to do."

That morning Mark searched for the word 'grace.' He learned that it is used a lot in Scripture and has a deep meaning. He saw that it has to do with God's kindness that flows from his love. He linked it with the favour the Lord gives even when we do not deserve it. He pondered some words he found: 'it is by grace you have been saved through having faith-it is not from yourselves, it is the gift of God - not by the things you do, so that no one can boast about what they have done.'

He knew that he had not deserved to be plucked from the treadmill of his previous existence. He understood that he had not asked for it. The Lord had decided to engineer it so he concluded that there would be purpose to what was going to happen, whatever that was going to be. He felt comfort in that. He did not feel ready to go back to the unit.

He searched for some songs with the word 'grace' that would match his contemplation. He found a song that had the words, "It's by grace I go free, you rescued me, now all I am belongs to you."

He found another that went, "Your grace is everything, more than I need." The song was sung by a woman. The voice was beautiful. He could not remember hearing a female voice in song before, but it reminded him of the warmth of the sunny days in the Nursery. That was the last time he could remember hearing the sound of a woman's voice. He played the songs over and over. It was like water to his thirsty soul.

That evening, over supper, they shared what they had found. Sanjay had explored more teaching on salvation. He shared that in ancient times, God had revealed to the people of Israel that, once a year, a sacrifice should be made. It would take away the sin of the people. The priest laid hands on a goat so that it took all the sin and then it was released into the wilderness, where it would likely die of exposure. Jesus died on a cross to pay once for all for all people in all time.

"It's amazing," he told them, "Jesus was the one with no sin who deserved to live. We all deserved to die for rejecting God's ways, but we live because he paid the price. There was no one else who could have done it. His sacrifice is our ticket to return to God. Another thing: in those days, if you were sold into slavery, your freedom had to be paid for by someone related to you. It could not be a stranger or a foreigner. Jesus is called the 'Lamb of God' and he is called the 'Son of Man'. He was fully human and fully God."

He paused then continued,

"We cannot earn salvation by doing something. We have to accept it as a gift. God reveals his severity in his judgment on us but he also reveals his love and generosity through the sacrifice and gift. It blows me away."

Johnson had spent time finding out about the Trinity.

"There are three – the Father, the Son and the Holy Spirit. They are all God and yet they are distinct. The Father always was and is in heaven. The Son came down and lived his life on earth for thirty-three years then returned to the Father. The Spirit comes from God. His job is to guide us and to lead us into truth. The thing that intrigues me is that they are three and yet they are one: incredibly close in relationship, knowing each other and in complete unity. In them, there is no separation, nothing hidden, nothing withheld," he said. "The thing that I have been pondering is that it says we are made in God's image. If God is relational, then we are meant to be in relationship with each other. Right?"

"There are some things which are revealed," said Michael slowly, "and there are some things which are a mystery, while we are in this life. When we get to heaven, we will know as we are known. That is going to be truly amazing. It is way beyond what we can imagine here and now. God knows us completely: our thoughts, our fears, our hurt, what we love, what our talents are. We are going to know, to a similar level, who we are, who God is, and what life on earth was all about: what happened and why it happened. And we will relate to each other as we were created to relate: in total love and complete truth."

The four men sat in silence for some minutes while they pondered these words.

Later that night, Sebastian arrived to lead them to the meeting. They filed out and made their way down the familiar route.

They reached a bay in a service corridor, with a line of bins. Michael halted and put his hand up.

"Something is not right," he whispered.

He gestured to them to hide in a recess behind the bins.

They waited.

Mark could hear his heart thumping in his ears.

Then he heard footsteps coming towards them down the corridor.

The footsteps stopped next to the bins.

A stiff, lean figure was standing next to Michael.

"What are you doing?"

The strange voice was abrupt; it cut the silence like a knife.

In the shadows, they held their breath.

Sebastian motioned to them to pray.

Mark found himself praying very simply: "help us."

"Just using this bin, Sir, medical waste," answered Michael.

The figure inspected the bin.

The head moved with jerky movements.

There was a strange, gurgling sound.

The figure suddenly doubled over.

"Oh cripes!" gasped the man, in desperation.

The weasel features of the face were contorted.

The man turned and fled down the corridor with two hands at his backside.

Michael stood by the bins until the sound of footsteps ended with a door slamming and silence.

"Did you see that?" Michael came to them with a hand over his mouth to try to contain his laughter. "What were you praying?"

"I just asked the Lord to make him go away!" replied Sanjay with a grin.

"It sounded like he had an attack of Delhi belly! He had the runs so he had to run!" said Michael.

They all laughed.

They carried on to the tunnel, still chuckling.

When they arrived at the meeting, the group was gathered in prayer.

They took their places in the circle.

After some time, John said, "We commit this meeting to you Lord. Come, Holy Spirit. Show us what you want to do tonight."

Mark heard different voices speaking.

"Jesus is here in the room with us"

"The Spirit is hovering over us."

"I see flames. The wind is fanning them so they burn stronger."

"He is saying, "Open your hearts to what I want to give.""

John said, "Let's respond in a time of worship. I believe tonight will be powerful."

They started with a song about inviting the Spirit to come as in days of old. Mark followed the words in the hologram. This song led into several more.

They were lifting up their hands during one of the songs when a strange thing happened. One man started to shake. Another man beside him abruptly fell flat on the floor. More men began to shake and vibrate. One man looked like he was a human pogo stick, bouncing on the spot. Mark felt warmth in his arms, and then his hands began to quiver. Soon his arms were shaking outside of his control. He could reduce it if he wanted but if he relaxed it got stronger. He was not alarmed because he somehow felt prepared for it. His knees went like jelly and he fell to the floor and had spasms of shaking.

Some of the men were struggling to stand up, some were chortling, some were hooting with laughter and more were catching it. The musicians had stopped playing and were slumped, heaving with spasms.

Mark's stomach muscles felt like they were doing cartwheels and a belly laugh started to bubble up from deep down. He closed his eyes, leant back his head and let it out. Laughter was filling the room. Many had tears of laughter in their eyes and seeing each other this way only seemed to make it stronger.

Another wave hit them and the few who were still standing fell down like they were ninepins, bowled over by an invisible ball. More laughter and hilarity followed. They all looked like a cheery bunch of drunks. When one of them tried to get up, others would stretch out and lay hands on them and they would stagger and collapse back to the floor, convulsing. More mirth and merriment resulted.

Eventually, it all calmed down and they sat in a circle, with a happy weariness and some chuckles.

"Do you understand what happened?" asked Steve, looking towards Mark, Johnson and Sanjay.

"I read that God gives joy, but I was not expecting it like that!" replied Sanjay with a wide grin.

"When you get a chance, read *The Acts of the Apostles*, from the beginning," said Steve, "you will find that when the Spirit came, the believers sometimes appeared like people drunk on wine."

Mark had never drunk anything alcoholic. Wine was never available to the units. He had heard about wine and drunkenness only at school, when they had been told about the 'decadence' of the times before the New Order. He had not properly laughed since he was a young child so it had been a strange yet wonderful experience.

When they parted, they hugged many of the other men of the group. They padded back towards the Sick Bay together. Michael met them at the exit from the tunnel. All was quiet in the corridors. They were all ready for bed so they bid each other goodnight.

Mark settled into bed. He felt happy, tired and ready for sleep in equal measures.

That night, his dream took him to a strange landscape. Many people were gathering in one place. There was anticipation, like something special was going to happen. He saw people of all ages, men and women. He looked into their faces. Each one was unique. He was struck by their hunger - not just a physical hunger but also a spiritual hunger. Mark had the feeling that something they needed was about to be given to them.

DAY 6

Mark awoke with a feeling that something new was going to happen.

There was so much to talk about over breakfast. They had all felt a wonderful sense of release in the laughter the night before.

Sanjay told of how he was one of the last standing and how he thought he had felt a little brush of wind before keeling over. He admitted that he had had some fear at letting the Spirit have His way.

Johnson said that he felt very safe. He felt so at home in this group. He felt like they were all like brothers. He loved this fellowship they were experiencing.

Mark told them that he had been plagued with the fear of being sent back to the unit, but that fear had evaporated with the laughter.

Michael said that they had had many meetings with similar events in the past. He could still remember what it felt like when it happened the first time for him. He felt that burdens were lifted off him. It was refreshing and liberating.

"The amazing thing to me is that the Lord touches every individual in a particular way," Michael added. "He knows our needs and what he wants to do in each one. For one person, it might be healing, for another it might be reassurance, for another it might be they are receiving a gifting. And he loves to do these things during our meetings, rather than when we are on our own. All of us are learning new things continually."

"What do you mean gifting?" asked Sanjay.

"A gift of something," replied Michael, "like a gift that enables you to do something - artistic work, writing, teaching, leading, caring for others, anything that the Lord might ask you to do."

They read together the section in *The Acts of the Apostles* where the Holy Spirit came on a large group of disciples in Jerusalem like a loud, rushing wind. Some people who saw them accused them of being drunk even though it was nine o'clock in the morning.

"That's just what we experienced!" said Sanjay.

They all agreed.

They split up to work separately. Sanjay researched the work of the Holy Spirit while Johnson hunted for teaching on the brotherhood of believers and on what fellowship is. Mark was drawn to learn more about worship.

Mark found that one of the first mentions of worship in the Bible was when Miriam, the sister of Moses, sang a song after the people crossed the Red Sea. He explored references to worship in the Law, at the time of King David, and the instruments they used in those days. He felt a yearning to understand at a deeper level why worship was given and what its purposes are.

When he came to share later, Mark told them, "I feel really drawn to worship. I am not sure what it is going to be at the moment. The more we worship at the meetings, the more I love it. I love listening to all sorts of songs. Today, I found a song which told a story of Jesus dying on a green hill far away."

"That song is an old hymn," said Michael, as he tapped on his screen, "it was written by an Irish lady in 1847, when she was sitting up late at night with her daughter who was sick. It says here that she wrote it for children."

"There were lots of different versions of it," said Mark.

He played the beginning of a song for them. It had an up-tempo drumbeat.

"Before the War of Unification, music was huge," said Michael, "there were thousands and thousands of bands. Britain and the United States had some of the most prolific songwriters. I think they led the way, with many others in places like Australia and South Africa. The church had a wide range of musicians in just about every style of music there was. The music industry was one of the many casualties of the war. The Executive only allows the type of music you heard in your units. You remember learning at school level how any independent music was against the Golden Rule?"

The others all nodded.

"In our meetings, everyone joins in the worship," said Mark. "No one forces them. We are musical, all of us. If we are made in God's image then I suppose God is musical. He must have created music."

Michael looked at him.

"You have learnt so much since you came here. It's marvelous to see. God works in a truly wonderful way," he looked at the others, "he is drawing each of you down the paths he has for you to walk. I am so happy to witness it. I hope I will see you in the future, when God has had opportunities to use you."

"You have been very kind to us," said Johnson. "I am not sure how we can thank you."

Mark and Sanjay agreed.

When Sebastian came they were all ready to leave. They made their way down the route that was now becoming familiar. There were several times where they had to wait silently, listening for any sound of Hansford. They heard footsteps but they were moving away. They waited then continued.

They reached the tunnel and pressed on, eager to reach the meeting.

Michael came with them.

When they entered the meeting room, they found the group of men in a huddle of prayer. The men stopped and looked up expectantly as they approached. They greeted them and their gazes were directed at Mark, Johnson and Sanjay.

John spoke first.

"Look you guys, we feel that this is a special night for you. We would like to direct our prayer to you tonight."

The three gestured to show that they were fine with the idea.

They took their places where John indicated, in the centre of the circle.

"Okay, let's get this prayer time started," said John, "come Lord by your Spirit. Show us what you want to do tonight. Give us ears to hear and eyes to see."

After a pause, some of the men took it in turns to speak:

"The Lord is saying he wants to fill you up."

"He is going to equip you."

"He knows the plans he has for you, to raise you up."

"I see rushing water, like a river. It is powerful."

"Let's lay hands on them. The Lord is going to work something important tonight."

Mark was kneeling with eyes closed. He felt many hands resting on his shoulders, arms and back. He could feel heat under the hands. He could hear voices but he could not make out the words. He felt something rising in his breast. It grew stronger. The feeling was a bit like bubbles and tingling. It was moving from his chest up towards his mouth.

"Something is happening, I am not sure what it is," he said frowning.

"You are receiving the gift of tongues, try speaking some expression in the Spirit. Join us as we pray."

The sound of the strange words was all around him. He opened his mouth and some words he had never used before came out. It was like making a connection in his spirit. He chuckled and tried again. More words poured out of his mouth. He had no idea what they meant but it did not seem to matter.

Similar things were happening to Sanjay and Johnson.

The men finished praying for the three individually and John asked them to sit together in the middle of the large circle. John said they would ask for prophetic words for them. Silence fell on the group as they waited.

Then Mark heard different men speak:

"Sanjay, the Lord is going to anoint your mouth for teaching."

"Sanjay, God is giving you authority. He is going to help you to be responsible with this gift."

"Johnson, God has given you a heart for your brothers. You are a pastor. God is going to use you to help the wounded."

"Mark, the Lord is anointing you for worship. Make it your goal to worship him in spirit and in truth."

"Johnson, God sees your heart. He is going to reveal his care for you. He says, "trust me always.""

"Mark, the Lord is going to give you songs for this time. Many people will see, many people will fear and many people will put their trust in the Lord."

"The Lord is reminding me of a picture I had before of you three as brothers. What he gives one of you will also bless the others. The more you share the more the Lord will bless you."

Then Mark heard John's voice saying, "I believe it is time to ask the Lord what the next move is for you three - is that okay?"

They opened their eyes and nodded. They bowed their heads and closed their eyes again.

"Lord," prayed John, "come and show us now, please reveal what you want these guys to do. What is the next move for them?"

With little hesitation, Mark spoke, "I see a picture of us in a small room, we are on something that is moving. It is dark outside. We are going somewhere through the night."

"He wants to take us somewhere out of the city," added Sanjay. "It's a safe place far from here."

"There are warrior brothers and sisters there," said Johnson. "I see them teaching us many things and equipping us."

They opened their eyes, intrigued.

"Does that sound right?" ventured Johnson.

There were grins on every face in the circle.

"It's what we expected," said John, "he wants to ship you out of the city and move you to the safe haven in the North. We have all been there. It is a wonderful place. We will take care of the arrangements. This time tomorrow you will be on your way. Tonight, we will say our goodbyes, until we meet again."

The three wanted to know more but John said it was better if they got back to the Sick Bay and rested for the journey. Michael would answer their questions in the morning.

"Before we go, let's break bread together," said John.

He explained about the Lord's last supper with his disciples while others went to fetch the bread and wine. They passed the cup and a tray of bread around the circle. Mark felt like the bond with the group was even stronger.

Then the men did something that Mark found very touching: they stood and formed a line and asked the three of them to start at one end so that they each had a chance to give them a hug and say a farewell. When Mark looked into their eyes, he marveled at the care and love he saw.

Sebastian and Michael led them back to the Sick Bay.

Mark did not want to go to bed but Michael promised them that they would discuss everything over breakfast.

That night, Mark had a dream where he was playing a strange game in the sunshine. He did not recognise the faces apart from Sanjay and Johnson. There was laughter. They were running on lush green grass, this way and that.

DAY 7

In the morning they were awoken by Michael bringing them breakfast.

"Boy o boy, you guys slept well," he chuckled. "Breakfast is an hour later than usual!"

Mark rose, washed his face and joined the others at the table.

"This morning, you can spend time in the ward," explained Michael. "You will leave late this afternoon. I will scan you out and Sebastian will take you to a loading bay and introduce you to the brother who will transport you to the rail depot. He will take you to meet the one who will look after you on the train to the North. You will have berths - like little rooms - so you will be able to sleep. It's a long journey and the train makes lots of stops throughout the night. When you get to your destination, someone from the safe haven will collect you."

A thought suddenly struck Mark: it was the mention of the loading bay. He recalled working in the observation rooms and watching people at work for hours at a time.

"What about the cameras in here? Have we been observed by other units? Will they not put alerts on us after what we have been doing?"

Michael smiled and shook his head. "That is all taken care of. When you first arrived, you were recorded over the first 24 hours. That footage has been manipulated and fed to the observation units."

"Who does that?" It was Johnson enquiring this time.

"I don't know much about it but we have people who are able to fix it. The church would not be able to operate in secret without them."

"Can you tell us more about the safe haven?" asked Sanjay eagerly.

"I went there when I was a new Christian," Michael paused and looked beyond them for a moment, "you will learn so much there. It is completely different to the city. It is hard to describe what it is like. There are woods that go on and on and fields and rivers. It is a farming area. You will hear bird song. I learnt to ride on a horse while I was there. The landscape is beautiful. When you are on the back of a horse, trekking through woods, the animals and birds do not seem to mind you so you can get really close to them.

"You will meet lots of people there. There is a team who stay there. Then there are people like you who go and stay. Some go for a short time, others for longer. You might have felt this was a holiday here, but the safe haven is beyond anything you have yet experienced. Often the Lord reminds me of things I saw there. You will love the fellowship and the worship times. You will love so many things about it.

"My advice is: take all you can from the experience. Spend time with many different people. Everyone there has things to share. They will help you seek the Lord as to what he wants you to learn.

"Now, excuse me because I have lots of things to do and I need to check that all the arrangements are being made. We'll talk later."

They did not protest when he took away the breakfast and left them to talk over the meeting last night.

Sanjay suggested they spend the morning searching on the gift of tongues and then share what they learn at lunch. The other two agreed.

Mark showered and dressed. He explored some teaching about the gifts of the Spirit. He found that there are many types. He wanted to know what the reason was for God giving this gift. He learnt that Jesus had promised the first Christians that the Spirit would teach them and guide them.

He listened to songs with the word 'Spirit' as he pondered.

Michael brought them lunch and left them to chat. They were excited about the next stage of the adventure. They had never been outside the city. They had only seen the countryside in images and in films on the screen.

Later on Michael and Sebastian came to them. They sat together with cups of tea and tasty cakes.

"Everything is ready," said Sebastian. "I am going to take you to the depot to rendez-vous with the cargo vehicle, which will take you to the rail head. The driver is called Jack. You will recognise him from the meetings. He will hand you over to the train guard. The train takes supplies across the country. There is a carriage for passengers. It has sleeping compartments. You are the only passengers tonight. Take these bags.

They have your supplies - some food, water, nightclothes and toothbrush. Keep them."

He handed them each a backpack. Mark had seen Workers wearing these packs when he had worked on observation.

"You will be met at the destination station. The guard is called Matt and he will make sure you meet the transport to the camp."

"Where are we going exactly?" asked Sanjay.

"The camp is located in Northern Scotland. The name of the area is Nairnside. It's a farming commune. The station where you will be met is called Nairn. It is about twenty-five kilometres East of a regional centre called Inverness."

"What about all the observation cameras?" asked Mark.

Sebastian answered, looking directly at him then the others.

"On the way over, we will blend in with the crowds," he said. "We will not walk together but you will follow each other in a string, with me leading. I will brief you at the necessary places. After I hand you over, Jack and Matt will look after you. There are very few cameras outside the city and none on the train to worry about."

"We have briefed the camp leaders about you," said Michael. "I have been in touch with them and so has John, so they know a bit about you and what you have experienced in the last week. They are really looking forward to meeting you tomorrow."

Sebastian looked at the clock.

"We should go in five minutes to coincide with the end of the afternoon session."

"Michael, Sebastian, we cannot thank you enough. This has been an incredible few days for all of us," said Johnson. "We will never forget what you have done for us. May the Lord bless you mightily for helping us."

Mark and Sanjay agreed.

"It has been an honour for us to serve you," said Sebastian.

"May you experience the love of the Lord in many ways," said Michael.

They made a huddle as Michael prayed for them briefly. He asked for protection and safety on the journey, and for healing and blessing at the camp.

He brought out the scanner and they took it in turns to scan out.

"You will report to Transport Depot 122 immediately," said the familiar voice.

They said their farewells to Michael and embraced him. Michael smiled broadly and told them that he would hear news of them.

The door closed behind them as Sebastian led them along the corridor to the main lifts.

"Keep about 10 metres between you and the person in front," he said, as they waited for the lift to take them down to the street level. "Walk and act like you are a Worker in your old unit. Don't look around. Remember when you were instructed to go to the Sick Bay? Walk like you walked on your way from the unit to here."

They left the Hospital Complex and headed towards the North. The streets were busy with Workers on the move. Mark kept his gaze on the ground ahead, glancing up regularly to check on Sebastian and Sanjay in front of him. He walked at the pace he had used for countless days in his block. He could feel his heart was beating. He kept his breathing steady.

They boarded a crowded tram, standing separately in the same carriage. They disembarked after six stops and walked across the street and into Transport Depot North.

They followed a route around to Bay 122. A black vehicle stood in the bay. From a side office, a figure beckoned them in. Mark gave a fleeting smile as he remembered the face from the church meetings. Jack greeted them.

"Hi, you guys! Welcome to the Depot. This is a big day for you."

Mark recalled the voice. He had heard that voice speak some prayers during the previous nights. He was able to relax: they were safe again.

Jack scanned them in. It was time for Sebastian to leave them. He gripped their shoulders in turn.

"The Lord be with you always," he said with fierce feeling.

They boarded the cab of the vehicle and Sebastian watched them move away, waving his last farewell.

Jack swung the vehicle onto a wide street and they drove to the North side of the city in the fading light. The buildings were not as tall as in the centre. Jack explained that they were passing accommodation blocks for Supervisors. Further on, they went through a heavy industry sector. Before long they turned into the Rail Terminus.

Mark was taken aback at the size of the vast shed with ranks of trains standing patiently. There were strings of lights high up under the roof structure. Jack pulled up in a space next to a platform and left them for a few minutes.

He came back with another man and gestured for them to join them.

The huge space was full of the sounds of throbbing engines and cargo being loaded.

"This is Matt," Jack had to speak over the din. "We will show you your carriage."

The train stretched for over 300 metres. There were all sorts of sections: enclosed goods trucks, open sections with vehicles and several low bed trucks with new tractors and machinery. There was a crane that straddled the train so that it could move the length of the train and load any of the trucks.

They followed Matt along to a carriage near the front. You could tell it was for passengers from the windows. They boarded and the heavy door slammed behind them, shutting out the noise outside. They were shown three compact sleeping compartments and a shared sitting area. It had a small kitchen to one side. They were surprised to find there were shower rooms along the narrow corridor.

"There are a few things I need to load with Jack, then I will join you here," said Matt. He checked his screen. "We are due to leave in twenty-three minutes."

They thanked Jack and he gave them a last wave.

The door slammed shut.

Mark, Johnson and Sanjay looked at each other.

"I am glad we are in this together," said Johnson.

"Me too," said Mark. "I don't think travelling on my own would have been much fun."

They chatted about their experiences since leaving the Sick Bay.

"It was strange to be among Workers heading back to their units," said Sanjay.

"Did anyone look at you?" asked Mark.

Johnson told them about one man on the tram that he thought was looking at him keenly. It made him feel uncomfortable but he had not said anything.

Before long, Matt came back. He was with two others. He introduced the driver and second guard. The driver was a big, stocky man with a chin covered in ginger bristles and a wide grin.

He shook their hands and said with an accent, "we are chuffed that we have the honour to take you lads North. Anything you need, just tell 'uz like, alright?"

They left, as it was time for the train to depart.

"Let's have a cup of tea and some supper," said Matt. He disappeared into the kitchen and came back with steaming cups and some food on a tray and set them on the table.

With a lurch, the train started to move forward into the night.

They dug into their backpacks and pulled out metal tins with insulated covers. The bottom layer had rice, the next layer had curry in a creamy brown sauce, and the top layer had a spicy vegetable mixture.

They sat around the table and Matt told them about his work on the railways as they ate. Their regular route was to the North but sometimes they went over to the continent. They had been to many of the megacities of Europe like New Hamburg, New Berlin and New Lyon, but only to the rail termini. He said that all the cities were built to the same design. Sometimes it was hard to spot the differences.

"When the train is fully loaded we do not reach high speeds. We will average about 60 kilometres an hour on some sections because we are heavily loaded. We have to stop at several stations to deposit cargo and take on other stuff. I will wake you at seven thirty in the morning so that you can get a view of the Scottish Highlands on our way up to Inverness. We are due in at Nairn at ten past nine."

"How did you get to join the church?" asked Johnson.

"It was those guys up at Nairnside. We met some of them when unloading there. They were praying for us before we knew anything about it. One day we were pulling into Nairn station and the engine just died on us. We had a stop-over while we had to wait for the repair team. They invited us to a meeting in Nairn. As soon as I walked in the door, I fell flat on my back! The Spirit just knocked me over. Then I laughed and laughed. I'll never forget it. When I was just about able to stand, they explained what was happening and they asked if I wanted to receive Jesus. We all got saved that night. The beauty of it was that we are a team so we have fellowship on our travels and the Lord uses us in many different ways, like ferrying you guys tonight."

Mark looked out of the window next to him. He had never seen the night like this. The landscape was a smudge of darkness with splashes of light passing for moments, then gone.

"Does it not get lonely?" he asked slowly.

"It used to, but not now."

Matt looked out of the window for some moments before he continued,

"When you are with the Lord, you're never alone again. We meet and pray together. The cool thing is that we visit churches all over the place. In every city, there is a church. The haven you are going to is not the only one. There is another in Wales and one in Ireland, and more in Europe. We are seeing the Lord add to our groups. It's brilliant."

The driver and the other guard returned.

"All's set," said the driver, "if I need to get back to ma' cab, I get an alert. Now, will you tell 'uz about your stories. We heard you joined only a week ago."

They shared their testimonies, starting with the units they were in and how they had met Sebastian, and ending with the leading to go North.

The crew listened closely, sometimes asking questions. When Sanjay told them about their encounter with Hansford in the bowels of the Hospital Complex, they chortled heartily.

Later on, the driver returned to the cab before their first stop. The train pulled into another large shed and the guards left them to oversee some loading, with more trucks shunted into position. It was getting late so they showered and got ready for bed.

Mark put his things in his berth then joined the others back in the lounge.

The train moved off again and the crew returned.

It was their turn to ask the crew about the day they came to salvation and about the different church groups they had met with in other cities.

Eventually, Matt suggested that they might want to get some rest. They would talk again over breakfast.

It was strange for Mark to have his own berth. Most of his life, he had slept in dormitories, surrounded by ninety-nine other boys. Sanjay and Johnson were the same. The berths had interconnecting doors so they opened them and locked them in the open position so they could chat before falling asleep. They took it in turns to pray. Sanjay went first, then Johnson.

"Lord, thank you for what you have done. Thank you that you have placed me with my brothers. You are so good to us and I love you for it."

"Father, I bless you for the amazing things you have done. I feel so grateful I can hardly put it in words. I trust you with whatever happens."

Mark felt relaxed. The stress of the day lifted.

"Thank you Lord that we are safe. Thank you for sending us away like this. I am really looking forward to tomorrow. Thank you for Jack and Matt and the others. You provide so much for us. Bless you."

The gentle swaying of the train was somehow comforting. They were like small children rocked to sleep in their cots. They slumbered peacefully and did not notice the many stops during the night: the shunting of more trucks; the cranes lifting off heavy cargo and depositing more bulky items.

Mark dreamt of a group of people: he could not see their faces. He felt very secure as a part of the group. They were standing and waiting for something. There was an extraordinary sense of unity. There was a moment when the waiting was over and they all knew what they were going to do. The feeling was a beautiful thing in itself: purpose, unity, destiny, readiness, and a sense of coming together to serve the Lord.

DAY 8

Matt woke them at 7.30 as he had promised. Mark opened his eyes. He got up and released the thick blind over the window. At first, he was dazzled by the intensity of the morning sunlight.

He gasped, wide-eyed.

He had never seen a sight like this before. There were smooth hills rising up from a wide valley in an earthy mixture of greens, browns, oranges and purples. The water in the river was a dark brown colour. He was looking at open moorland spreading out for miles. The morning light was crisp and pure.

The train had passed the high point of the Drumochter Pass in the Cairngorm mountains. There were only a few buildings scattered among tall pine trees along the widening valley. Mark had never seen open land before with his own eyes. He blinked and struggled to accept that it was real.

Sanjay and Johnson had opened their blinds. The effect was profound on each of them. They stood in silence at their windows, gazing out.

Music started playing, filling their cabins. Matt had chosen a worship song with some deep Celtic undertones. What his ears heard and what his eyes saw combined so that it touched Mark deep down in his soul. He could not put it in words. Perhaps his soul had yearned for years to perceive the beauty of creation.

The realisation that God had created this landscape with such beauty was overwhelming. Tears welled in Mark's eyes. He had to keep wiping them because they made the landscape melt into a blur.

Two silent tears streaked down Sanjay's face. Johnson let the tears drip from his jawline.

Then a haunting song started playing.

It was about someone saying farewell to their homeland, to obey the call of God to a far away land:

"Here I am, on the edge of the world with you."

The tears flowed freely now for all three of them.

The song matched the feeling they each had that they had left forever all that was familiar and secure. Their lives in the units had been all they had known, and here they were on a journey into the unknown. They had heard that same quiet voice inviting them to move out to the far away. To put their trust in someone they could not see. For them, it was the edge of the world.

Matt opened the door.

"I just love that song. I have got breakfast ready. Just come in your pyjamas if you want to, guys."

Mark splashed water on his face. Each berth had a sink with a hinged cover, under the window. He rubbed his face with a towel and looked at his reflection in the mirror. He studied himself like he was seeing himself for the first time.

His hair was still short. His skin was pale from lack of exposure to sunlight, but his eyes had a clarity and brightness that he had not noticed before. There was calmness in his countenance.

"Welcome to a new day in your new life," he said to his reflection.

Matt had cooked eggs, tomatoes and mushrooms. The table was laid and there was toast already buttered and cups of milky tea. The driver and guard arrived and sat down.

"How did you sleep?" asked the driver.

"Like a baby," said Johnson.

"Rocked to sleep!" added Sanjay.

This breakfast smells delicious," said Mark.

"What do you make of the moors of Scotland?" asked Matt.

"Beyond words," said Sanjay. "I've never seen anything like it."

"Those first two songs were very moving," said Mark. "It got the waterworks going before breakfast."

"Well, I love hearing those songs with that view of the moors," said Matt. "Sometimes I sit here and have a good bawl myself."

Sanjay asked the driver how he could leave the cab while the train was moving. The driver explained that the speed of the train was centrally controlled. He was required to feed information back to the control centre at certain points. The railway line was cut over one hundred and fifty years ago, he told them.

They passed a ruin on a hill: bare walls and no roof, like the bones of an old fort. They passed small villages then crossed a wide river. The fields were populated with sheep and cattle with thick winter coats. Narrow roads twisted along the valley, stringing the villages together. Some children standing on a fence waved as they sped past.

The train followed beside a wide, empty road then slowed to a stop. A sign told them the name of the place: 'Aviemore.'

They cleared breakfast then dressed and returned to the lounge to stare out of the windows.

Before long, the train got underway again.

It was like watching a movie: they sat still while the view constantly changed. Things close to them flashed past, things in the distance gradually showed different angles. Mark found it mesmerizing. They spotted different things while Matt pointed out villages, the major summits, and gave them many of the names. He explained how this area had been the home of different clans over the centuries - each with its territory.

Every village had an old church. They looked empty and unused but they spoke of a time when faith in God was normal.

They were now climbing up another summit through cuttings, hewn long ago into the hard, dark rock, then the train coasted as they dropped down towards Inverness.

They left the roads and the line took them through dense forests of pines and birch trees. At the foot of many of the trees, there were lush greens - delicate mosses. Mark wondered what animals lived in the hidden places among the woods.

They swept over a high viaduct as the line crossed another river valley.

"We will be down in Inverness in less than fifteen minutes," said Matt.

They had glimpses of the coast in the distance between the cuttings and the trees.

Matt explained that the farmland was more fertile near the coast. The high ground was covered in snow in winter. Sometimes the line was closed if the snowdrifts were too deep.

The train slowed as it approached Inverness station and came to a halt. Without delay, cranes began to lift some of the cargo, which included farm machinery. The train was loaded with timber, wool and frozen fish.

After a time, the train set off along the coast towards the East.

"Next stop, Nairn!" called Matt.

They put all their things, few as they were, in their bags, tidied their berths and pulled on their boots.

The train slowed and pulled up in a small station next to a timber yard.

They stepped out.

Mark noticed that it was cooler here than back in the city. They breathed in deep the fresh air. The sky seemed very blue between the puffy clouds.

The driver and the guard came up and said goodbye.

Matt led them over to a large transport vehicle parked next to a goods truck. He introduced them to a man called Stevie.

The roof of one of the train trucks lifted up and a crane picked up crates of boxes, bags and packages and set them down next to the vehicle. A forklift truck set the crates neatly down on the rear of the vehicle.

Stevie gave Matt a package with some of the fresh produce from the farm.

"I expect we will see you guys again," said Matt to them as he shook their hands. They thanked him for looking after them.

Matt waved to the driver and climbed aboard the train.

The train engine throbbed and they watched it move off.

They waved at Matt until he was out of sight as the train made a slight left turn, crossing a river bridge.

When it had disappeared, Mark could hear the wind and the call of birds.

"Alright guys, let's take you to the camp," said Stevie. His voice had an accent a bit like the train driver.

There was space in the cab for all of them. Stevie moved off onto the road, turning right, away from the coast.

"The air smells different here," said Mark, sitting by the open window.

"You'll have smelt the sea coz' the beach is just the other side of the town," replied Stevie, with a gesture towards the North.

The road led towards the South, out of the town and past fields then crossed the river and along the South side of the floodplain. They could see the land rise in a series of ridges, mostly covered in forest, with bare moorland beyond on the high ground.

They passed one field where three tractors were working. Excited seagulls flapped in their wake, searching for worms in the newly turned, rich, brown soil.

Stevie gave them a commentary on the land-scape as they glided along: the crops in the fields, the river they crossed, and the woodland they passed.

They pulled off the road, drove into the farm centre and came to a stop.

There were large sheds with farm machinery: tractors, ploughs, seed drills, and three giant combine harvesters.

Stevie pointed. "Over there are the cattle sheds."

Stevie used a forklift truck to unload most of the crates into the nearest shed.

They climbed back into the vehicle and drove on, turning South up the hill.

Stevie swung the truck into a large yard and eased the vehicle carefully into a shed and closed the door behind them. They all got out and unloaded the rest of the cargo.

Stevie opened a door at the rear.

"Welcome to the camp," he said, leading them up a track past rows of huts, into a large clearing.

Above them was spread a thin, gossamer fabric that allowed the light to filter through.

People were emerging into the clearing from every direction. They came and welcomed the three newcomers. Soon they were surrounded by a crowd of friendly faces. Mark was surprised to see that there were men, women and children, from the young to the old. They were dressed in a range of clothes. They did not all conform to one uniform like the Workers in the city. Some had long hair. Their faces had healthy colour from time spent outdoors.

A tall, slender man in his thirties came through the circle and greeted Stevie. A black Labrador was by his side.

"Hi guys, I am Jasper. I help run this place."

He shook each hand firmly, looking into every eye.

"It's great you have come. I heard a bit about you from Michael, Sebastian and John. They have all been here. Let me show you around. There is quite a bit to see."

He turned to the crowd and raised his voice.

"Thank you all for making them welcome. I expect we will hear more at the meeting tonight."

The people smiled and dispersed, taking with them the murmur of their voices.

They perched on some benches on the edge of the clearing. The dog licked Mark's hand.

"We set up this camp about two years after the war," explained Jasper. "We started small.

Today, we have two hundred and seventy people on site. More of our people live in the local villages. We are here to serve the churches and help anyone the Lord sends us, in every way we can. This is our camp meeting place. We usually meet most nights for sharing, prayer and for worship, a bit like the meetings you have been to back in the city. Tonight, if you are up for it, we would like to ask you to share how you came to faith and how you came here. Testimonies are very encouraging. I am sure you have heard stories that helped you. God often uses them in lots of ways. Many people here have prayed for you. What do you think?"

"I would be happy to share," said Johnson without hesitation.

"How long would you like us to speak for?" asked Sanjay.

"It's up to you. Maybe a few minutes? We have located some footage of you doing your normal work in your units, before you met Sebastian. We would like to show some, if that's okay?"

"We have received so much from others, I would be happy to give something back," said Mark, "although I have never spoken to a large group before."

"Everyone here is for you," replied Jasper reassuringly. "We would really appreciate it. We sow in prayer, like a farmer who plants seed. Hearing your stories will help us to keep going and not give up."

Looking at Jasper as he spoke, Mark liked him immediately. He had a warm and easy way about him. There was a sureness about him, like he knew who he was and what he was doing. It reminded him of John.

A thought came to him.

"Jasper." Mark said the name slowly. "The worship guys back at the church mentioned someone called Jasper. They said he had taught them a song, I think. Was that you?"

Jasper smiled. "Yes, I taught them a bunch of songs when they came up. Now, let's start our tour. I want to show you as much as we can fit in before lunch."

They started with the huts surrounding the meeting place. They were set out in clusters. There was a cluster of huts for teaching groups. There was a communication hub with people working among banks of computer screens. There were workshops around a yard given over to mechanical work, where people in overalls were working on various vehicles, contraptions and machinery.

There was the shed where Stevie had parked the transport vehicle. Some of the sheds were for storage, some were full of vehicles.

"How come you have so many vehicles?" asked Sanjay.

Jasper grinned. "Some were scrapped. We salvaged them and fixed them up. Some we have modified. Some we have, well, borrowed. We have talented people passing through here. Everyone works together and it's amazing what wisdom the Lord gives us. Plus it's fun. Just you wait 'til you get a go. The motorbikes will give you a kick, I bet!"

"What is that fabric over the camp?" asked Sanjay, pointing upwards.

"We call it the Chameleon covering. It makes us invisible to satellites, cameras and radar. We are hidden."

Mark looked at him.

"You mean the New Order can't see us?" he asked.

"Yup," came the reply. "It's a prototype. It was consigned and we… well we kind of borrowed it."

Jasper grinned at them.

They passed more huts and came back to the meeting place and continued beyond it. There was an old, stone wall to the left side and a line of tall trees to the right. The track had brought them to a gap and Jasper stopped.

They came to a halt next to him and looked up.

There, in front of them, was a green lawn and beyond it there stood a castle, with a tall tower rising up above the trees. Mark had a moment of wondering if he was dreaming again. The tower had battlements and round turrets at its four corners. The stone had been weathered by many winters. The window panes had slender strips of white timber. Some openings were thin and narrow. There were wings of the building around the tower at the centre.

"Is that... real?" Sanjay stumbled over the words.

"It's very old. My dad lived here when he was a boy. His father's family had been here for generations. My dad brought us up here on holiday lots of times. After the war, I came up here and I applied to join the Nairnside commune. I was eighteen. Most people headed for the cities. A few of us asked the Lord what he wanted us to do. He showed us that he wanted us to serve him right here. He gave us visions of a camp. He told us that people would come here from afar to learn more of him and more about themselves: like an oasis in the wilderness, and a base for mission. When I think about what the Lord has done over the years, sometimes I want to celebrate, sometimes I just want to cry."

They walked across the lawn.

There were some old trees standing in lines on both sides like sentries. To the North, the ground sloped gently down then flattened out. There were gardens of fruit and vegetables stretching in both directions. There were large areas covered with clear membranes. Beyond was the floodplain with the farm.

"We grow much of our own food," continued Jasper. "In those covered sections, we grow plants that would normally not survive this far North. Now let's go and have tea."

He led them up to the gate of the castle, across a drawbridge that swayed as they crossed, under a gateway, through a paved courtyard and down some stone steps into a second courtyard. They entered through the main door - a large and heavy timber door with an iron handle that made a loud clunk as Jasper lifted the latch.

Inside, they paused in the narrow hall.

Mark liked the smell of the place. The aroma had a mixture of polish, timber, flowers and leather. The carpet had a pattern of green, black, blue and red. Jasper explained that it was called tartan. On the white washed walls, portraits of tight-lipped ancestors peered down at them.

At the foot of the main stairs there was an old clock with an ornate face on a shelf. Suddenly it chimed beside them. The sound was crystal clear in Mark's ears. The place seemed to ooze history.

Jasper stooped to open the door of the dining room and led them in.

The room had tall windows along one wall and large tapestries on the other three walls. They had an assortment of strange figures, some on horseback and a line of windmills. Some of the faces were grotesque. At the far end of the room was a generous fireplace with a wide, carved stone over the whitewashed hearth. The table was covered in a crisp linen cloth. They went over to the windows. There was a wide stream below, the bare rock of a small cliff and towering trees above. Small birds flitted in the branches. A bird table covered in breadcrumbs attracted the birds to the window sill and the branches nearby. They were delighted to catch sight of the birds close up before they darted away.

Two more people came in and they turned to greet them.

"Hi guys, I am Jonathan. This is my wife, Helena."

Jasper introduced them. Mark immediately felt this older couple were like family. He felt at ease and safe. The anxiety of the journey lifted.

They sat down and Jasper poured from the white teapot that was sitting on a hot plate. He handed out some thin biscuits.

They looked at them curiously.

"Oatcakes," said Jasper, "they are a traditional Scottish biscuit."

Mark bit into his and crunched it between his teeth.

"How was your journey?" asked Helena. Her eyes were warm and her manner was like a mother to them.

They took it in turns to describe all the stages of the journey from the city. The highlight for each of them was opening the blinds and seeing the moors for the first time. Johnson mentioned how they had wept at the sight.

"You have been stuck in the city all your lives like many others who have come here," said Helena caringly, "they all received much healing here. I hope you will too."

"Did Jasper ask you whether you would share tonight at the meeting?" enquired Jonathan. Mark thought he was direct with his question in the way a person is when they are in authority.

Johnson spoke for them and said that they would be fine to do so.

"Have you got any questions you want to ask now?" asked Jonathan.

"I have one. How did you come to be here?" asked Johnson politely.

Jonathan and Helena explained how, before the war, they were friends with Jasper's parents. They used to live in a house in England with their two children. During the war, they went into hiding in a remote spot in Scotland. The Lord had shown them the camp in a series of dreams and visions. They travelled here, met Jasper and helped set it up. The camp had grown as the Lord sent them more people. Their son and daughter were away in America on a mission.

"We have people who were based here, who we send out to other cities or countries, as the

Spirit leads us," said Jasper. "The Lord has plans for every child of his. One of the things we want to help you with is to understand the Lord's will for you. You are welcome to stay here as long as you want to."

"You said that you prayed for us. How did you even know anything about us?" asked Mark, raising his eyebrows.

Helena explained.

"We are in contact with lots of churches. As soon as you went to the ward in the hospital, the church alerted us. We have people who pray daily while the rest are working. They are called the Intercessors. We called a prayer meeting of the whole camp community that afternoon. We prayed for a few hours so that your first meeting was bathed in prayer. Church groups in other countries joined us in praying for you. In the days after, John sent us updates of your progress. You see, we are one church, one family."

"That's why so many people came out to greet you when you arrived," interjected Jasper. "We asked the Lord if he would send you up here, before you prayed with John and the others."

"That's amazing," remarked Sanjay.

"And touching," said Johnson.

"I am not sure how we can thank you," added Mark.

It was Jonathan's turn to speak. He spoke with confidence, like he was used to groups of people listening to him, and with some brevity, as a man who has wants to make the most of his time.

"The Lord has his hand on you. We are very excited to have you here. I am looking forward to spending time with you guys. You will have opportunities to learn together. Now Jasper has some more to show you, including where you are staying. We will see you later on."

He winked at Jasper. Mark was curious: he had never seen someone wink before.

They got up, and went out the way they had come in.

Across the drawbridge, Jasper turned right and opened a large timber door in the old stone wall. The door creaked on its hinges. On the other side there was a walled garden with long lines of flower beds, deep green hedges and closely cut lawns. They walked through the garden and through an iron gate.

They passed a canteen block. Jasper explained that they would have their meals there. The ground beyond sloped uphill. There was a long building built into the slope. Its roof was grass. Beyond the grass, higher up the hill, at the edge of the field, there was a stone dyke with countless tall trees behind it, the edge of a large wood.

They entered through a wide door into a passage that ran straight ahead then turned to the left and right, underground.

"This is the men's sleeping quarters." Jasper said as he turned left and led them along the long passage.

Light filtered from above through rooflights. He paused outside a room labeled 'Mizpah' with their names on a label below. He opened the door. The room had windows out towards a large green field and the meeting place beyond.

"You should change. Here is your new kit."

He gestured to clothing neatly folded on each bed, with a name label placed on each. Mark went over and inspected his new outfit. The code on the breast was different: G1L3E290718 RN052RCC3 (Generation 1; Level 3; Europe; 29 July 2018; Register Number 052; Region C; Community 3).

"In the cupboard you will find more clothes. It gets cooler at night so you'll need the jackets," said Jasper.

They left their bags in the room then Jasper showed them the showers and washroom down the passage. They went outside and walked back towards the castle. Jasper led them across a bright blue footbridge that reached over the stream. They climbed the far bank and Jasper showed them the village. The women's quarters were dug into the bank. Jasper explained that the old houses in the village were used by families. Many people who lived in the village before the war, left for the cities. The house on the corner was the medical centre. Jasper said he wanted to introduce them to someone. He opened the door and a woman in a nurse's dress stood up from a desk.

"Hi Jazz, are these the new lads?" asked the woman.

"Mark, Sanjay, Johnson, this is Rachel. She's from Liverpool."

"Heard a good bit about yous," said Rachel, smiling. Her accent was strong.

"Rachel, where is Immy? She wanted to meet these guys."

"I'll call her. We've got two kids with the mumps."

Rachel opened the inner door and called, "Ay, Im', get 'ere."

A pretty woman with blonde hair and bright blue eyes emerged. She was of a similar age as Jasper.

She came up to them and Mark noticed tears starting to fill her eyes. Without saying anything, she touched each one on the cheek, looked closely at their faces and then held each one in an embrace. When she got to Mark, he could feel her shudder as they hugged. There was something special in her touch. Mark could not say what it was: it was warm and soothing.

Jasper put his arm across her shoulders. She looked weak at the knees so he helped her to sit down.

"Immy is my sister," he said. "You guys are very special to her. Well, you're special to all of us but her the most. She has waited a long time - half her life - for this moment."

Imogen nodded, still unable to speak.

"You're making a right mess, petal," said Rachel, and handed her some tissues.

Imogen pointed to the bookshelf. Rachel passed a well-used photo album to Jasper.

Jasper leafed through some pages.

"Imogen used to work in a Nursery in the city many years ago in the early years of the New Order. She nursed baby boys; lots of them. It was a long time ago, before she came here to help build the camp."

He held the book so that Mark could see the page. At the top, it had a large title word: 'Mark.' The page was filled with pictures of a young boy.

"It's you," said Imogen in a low voice, wiping her tears.

Mark looked at her, searching her face, unsure what she meant. There was something about her voice that was familiar to him.

"I remember a nurse. She used to sing to me in my bed," said Mark.

Imogen let out another sob and nodded. She wiped her nose and eyes.

"That was me," she said, her voice quavering and faltering. "You only had a number. No name. I asked the Lord to show me what your name was. He told me your name was Mark. I used to sing to you as you went to sleep. I used to pray for you as you slept. I asked the Lord to save you and show you the truth about who you are."

"Imogen is the one who kept on insisting, year after year, that we pray for three boys called Sanjay, Johnson and Mark," said Jasper.

He turned back a page and showed it to the three of them: the page on one side was entitled

'Sanjay' and on the other, 'Johnson.' He handed the book to them so that they could study the images.

Imogen said that she learnt their names the same way but she was faced with a dilemma.

"I felt I could not pray for all the boys to a deep level so I asked the Lord to show me which boys he wanted me to focus most of my prayers on," continued Imogen.

Sanjay, Johnson and Mark had not seen photographs of themselves before. The clothes they were wearing in the images started to bring memories flooding back. They sat down speechless, struggling to take in the news.

"I can hardly put in words how much joy it gives me to know that the Lord heard our prayers. And now you are here," said Imogen as she sat with them.

"You're a right trooper, Im' petal," added Rachel, touching her arm.

Sanjay, Johnson and Mark all sat motionless. It started to dawn on each of them: they had been so lonely and abandoned for so many years; they had not known human care and love; they had been like orphans in a harsh place, like prisoners held captive. The truth of what they had been through came to them.

They started to weep quietly.

Rachel, Jasper and Imogen sat with them and held them.

Sanjay, Johnson and Mark wept from the depth of their hearts.

Mark felt a range of emotion: aching pain because of the rejection and harsh treatment; relief that those years were over; sadness at the years that were lost; mourning for what could have been.

Eventually the tears eased and the burden lifted.

The small device in Jasper's pocket came to life.

"It's time we went for lunch in the team dining room, in the castle," said Jasper gently. "Let's go up there."

"I'll stay here just in case," said Rachel. "I'll see yous later."

They got up and ambled back across the blue bridge and up to the castle.

Imogen told them about her excitement when the news came through that three men called Sanjay, Johnson and Mark had joined the church in New Birmingham. She had waited to see images of them although she knew in her heart that it was them. She had leapt for joy when she had seen their faces on the screen.

They went through a courtyard on the South side and into a less formal dining room. They went up to the counter to choose their food. Jasper introduced them to the team on catering.

They sat at a large table. They were joined by Jonathan and Helena. Stevie and another man came in and took their places.

Jasper said to them, "this is Pete, he is going to be your guide with Stevie. They will make sure you find your way around for the next week or so."

"Our rooms are close to yours," said Pete, "we will keep you right. If there is an E. Vac, we will lead you."

"E. Vac stands for Emergency Evacuation," said Jasper. "If we come under attack, we will disperse in different directions. Don't worry about it for a second. We will take care of everything."

"How was it for you meeting our nurse?" asked Helena, gesturing towards Imogen with a smile.

They described what had happened in the medical centre.

"It's still sinking in," said Johnson. "It seems incredible. Yesterday, I had no connection with those early years. It's a bit like finding family I never knew I had. I feel like crying really helped. I needed to let out those emotions which have been bottled up for so many years."

"The first time Imogen hugged me, I felt something. I can't explain it," added Mark. "It was the first time a woman has hugged me since I was five."

"Do you feel like you received some healing?" asked Helena.

Sanjay, Johnson and Mark all nodded.

Helena got up and gave each one a hug.

They wiped the new tears that ran down their cheeks.

"Tell us more about the Nursery," asked Sanjay, turning to Imogen.

Imogen described the set up there. She explained that the nurses were trained not to develop any personal attachment to the children. She said she knew in her heart that she could not do that. She asked the Lord to show her ways to love the children without it being picked up by the surveillance cameras. She used to touch them and hold them as often as she could. She would whisper to them. She would pat their little bottoms. She would whisper words of scripture to them. She often used to take night shifts so that she had time alone in the ward when she could hold them and sing to them and pray over them. Sanjay had been the first child she had felt the Lord prompt her to pray for. Johnson arrived three months later and Mark followed the next quarter. She worked in the Nursery for four years before the boys were moved on to the school complex. She then felt the Lord direct her to come North after that.

"I never forgot about you," she added. "I held onto the hope that the Lord heard our prayers."

They finished lunch and Mark felt revived.

Jasper suggested they go to the Communications Centre. They met the team who were based there. Jasper asked the three if they wanted to find out about their records.

"We can access your files and if you want to find out who your parents are, we can do that."

Mark looked at the other two.

"What do you think?" he asked uncertainly.

Johnson was the first to make a decision.

"Yes, can I do that?" he said.

They sat him down at one of the screens. Mark and Sanjay stood behind him. One of the team typed in his code number and up came his file. He was born on April 19th in the year 2017.

"Hey, look," said Imogen, "today is your birthday! Happy birthday, Johnson."

"How old am I?" asked Johnson, staring at the screen wide-eyed.

"You are eighteen today!" said Jasper.

They scrolled down to find details about his parents. Both had numbers and profile images.

"Let's print these off for you." Jasper handed him the images.

Sanjay went next at another terminal. He learnt that he was born on January 21st 2017. He was eighteen.

Mark sat at a terminal. He discovered that he was born on July 29th 2017. He was seventeen. He studied the faces of his parents on the print out sheets. He felt that he had a strong look of his father.

"Your parents have probably never seen you," explained Jasper. "They take sperm from healthy males and insert them into females chosen for good genetic combination. Your parents probably never even met. They tell them nothing. They do not get to see their children."

"It says here they are in units in New Birmingham," said Mark.

"That's right," said Jasper, "but there are over 12 million people in that megacity. You might have walked right past your father two weeks ago and he might have not even noticed you. Remember, everyone is drugged. Their perception is reduced."

"What are they doing now, do you think?" asked Mark.

"I don't know but we could see, if you want to," replied Jasper.

Jasper showed Mark how he could type in his father's code number and up came a surveillance screen, like the one he was used to. He saw a room of figures packing crates in a warehouse. There was one figure dressed as a Supervisor who was flagged. Mark zoomed in. He watched intently. He gently touched the screen, like he was stroking the figure.

Mark typed in his mother's code. He had never seen a unit of women at work before. They had only been permitted to view other male units. The scene that came up was a laundry very similar to the one he had worked in. The slender figure that was flagged was another Supervisor. She was checking the women working at the lines of washing machines. He watched her every move for a long while. What did her voice sound like, he wondered.

"Guys, it's time to break for tea." There was something very soothing to Mark about Imogen's voice. It helped with the sense of sadness he felt after seeing his parents.

Mark looked up. Imogen and Jasper had stood back and left them to stare at the screens. Mark did not know how much time had passed. They had been engrossed.

"You can come back here tomorrow," reassured Jasper with a smile.

Imogen and Jasper led them to the canteen where many of the camp had gathered for drinks and snacks.

"After tea break most days, we play games before getting ready for supper," explained Jasper. "We would like to teach you to play too."

They met some of the other men who had rooms in their sleeping quarters. Between there and the huts around the meeting place, there was a wide area of grass. Men and women and some children were kicking a ball.

"This game is called football," called Jasper as he led them over to join in. "It has been played in this country for centuries. There are two teams. You try to move the ball into the opposition's territory. You score a goal by kicking it into that net over there." He pointed. "You are not allowed to handle the ball unless you are the goalkeeper. You can use your forehead and chest. Come and have a go."

Sanjay, Johnson and Mark stood by and watched with interest at the players running, passing and tackling. One team had blue bibs, the other red.

"I seem to remember that we played with a ball when we were in the Nursery," said Mark.

The red team had fewer players and called to them to join their team. Pete handed them red bibs and they tentatively walked onto the pitch. The ball passed across to a boy who came running towards Mark and dodged past him. He turned and watched Stevie run alongside and kick the ball over the sideline. They retreated to help defend the throw-in. A loose ball came to Sanjay and he swung his leg, sending the ball up the field. He laughed.

"This is great," he said with a wide grin.

Pete beckoned to Mark to move forward. The ball came to him and he carefully controlled it then sent it in a wide arc to a player on the left side.

"Lovely pass," called Jasper.

It was strange to them to use their bodies in this way but the more they played, the more they grasped: balance, understanding, ability. There were some air shots, when they misjudged the speed and bounce of the ball, but the shouts of encouragement from the others spurred them on to keep trying.

Mark was struck by a sudden thought. There was something familiar about this moment. He could not place it and carried on playing. He had seen this before.

Eventually, a whistle blew and the blue team celebrated a 5-3 win. They all gathered and shook hands.

Mark was breathing heavily and sweating.

"That was so much more fun than any of the exercise sessions back in the unit," he said.

The others agreed.

They went with Pete and Stevie back to the men's quarters for showers and to change. They found the clothes in their room fitted well. They sat on their beds and traded memories of the day.

"Could you believe that castle?" said Sanjay.

"I had no idea old buildings like that still existed. This is quite a place, like Sebastian and the others said." added Mark.

"Everyone is so friendly here, it's like at church back in the city," said Johnson, "but with fresh air. I wonder what Sebastian is up to now. It might be pretty quiet on the ward for Michael. I hope we'll see them again before long."

Stevie and Pete arrived and they headed in the direction of the canteen. The light was fading in the Western sky. The birds had retreated yet Mark could still hear one calling in the woods.

They found a table. Jasper and Imogen came and joined them, as did Helena, Jonathan and Rachel. They ate a healthy supper. The game had given them an appetite.

Jasper explained that they had learnt to play games when they were at school, as all children did back then.

"Before the War, football was huge in just about every country in the world. The best foot-ballers were famous and were paid enormous sums of money. People used to be passionate about following a team. There were so many arguments about which teams were the best. There was a special group of 20 top teams in England. Every year they would all play each other and the team at the top, at the end of the season, would receive a big cup.

"My dad supported Everton," said Rachel in her accent, "but some of me family supported Liverpool. It was right friendly like."

Jasper grinned at her.

He continued, "Every four years, there was a competition between the best countries for the World Cup. Even at school, we had teams, and we used to play other schools."

"Girls played games as well," said Imogen. "We played games like netball and hockey. If you come over to the women's side, we can show you."

"We play footie too," chipped in Rachel, "when we're in the mood but."

"There's so much to show you!" said Jasper.

Suddenly, Mark put his hand to his head. They turned to look at him. "There was a moment in the match when I thought 'this looks familiar'. Now I remember: a few nights ago I had a dream - there were people running on grass, playing a game I did not understand.

The moment in the match was the same as the moment in the dream!"

"That is called *deja vu*, which means 'already seen'," said Imogen. "There have been times when God gave me a dream as a preview of what I was going to witness. I think it's a way he confirms to us that we are in His will."

"That's right," said Jasper, "God showed me this camp in dreams long before the first people came here."

Jonathan and Helena nodded.

"You said people were paid money to play football, "said Sanjay thoughtfully. "What is money?"

"Good question," answered Jonathan. "We'll try and explain it tomorrow. But now let's talk about tonight."

They discussed what they might be willing to talk about at the meeting.

"They will love anything you share," said Imogen encouragingly.

They had finished eating and they cleared their table. Pete and Stevie went to check on preparations for the meeting while the rest loitered among the sofas next to the dining area. The light was fading and the evening sky was suffused with a deep dark blue overhead. The trees stood as tall silhouettes against a swathe of light green from the last of the sunlight. Mark could not remember ever being under a clear sky at the end of the day.

"Isn't it beautiful?" said Helena, noticing his quiet gaze.

"Our friends back in the city could not have put in words what this is like," he said. "Do you get this every night?"

"The light changes all the time up here. The air is very pure and unpolluted. During the winter, we don't sit out like now. It's too chilly, so we have the sun room." She pointed to a building with a slanting glazed roof.

It was time to go to the meeting.

Imogen took Mark's arm as they strolled over.

"I am so delighted you guys are here," she said. Mark smiled into her eyes. He felt like she was a big sister: someone who knew him and cared for him deeply from when he was young.

They arrived in the meeting area and Jasper showed them where they could sit. People were arriving from nearby villages. There were some young boys taking it in turns to jump off the central raised area. One little boy, with curling fair hair and lovely dark eyes, came up to him.

Mark found himself smiling when he heard his young voice.

"Hello. What's your name?" asked the little boy, looking up at him.

"I'm Mark. I arrived today."

"How old are you? I'm seven years old."

"I'm seventeen," replied Mark, "I found out today."

"Will you come and visit us in our school?" asked the boy.

"I would like that a lot," said Mark with a grin.

"Good," said the boy, and skipped away to play.

Jonathan, Helena, Imogen and Jasper stood up on the stage and welcomed everyone. They mentioned their three new guests and invited Sanjay to join them. The crowd responded with clapping, whistles and some calls. On the screens they showed the figure of Sanjay in his unit. When Jonathan prompted him, Sanjay described how he had met Sebastian and how he had been transferred to the Medical ward.

They showed some scenes filmed in the church meetings. There were the three of them looking uncertain at the first meeting; Sanjay surrounded by praying men; then Sanjay listening intently at the sharing in a later meeting. They had some footage from the night when they fell about laughing under the Holy Spirit. The crowd called out and clapped to show their approval. Some of the scenes were comic and everyone laughed when they saw some of the figures staggering and falling down.

Helena asked Johnson to join her and invited him to share how he had joined the church while they showed some highlights of his, including him joining in the sharing in a meeting.

Jasper beckoned to Mark.

He went up and said, "Hi everyone, I am Mark."

The crowd responded with clapping, some hooted and made a noise.

Mark's knees felt a little shaky.

Jasper turned to him, "Mark, will you share about how it all started for you and tell us about your dream?"

They showed some observation footage of Mark asleep in his unit. He was curious to see himself on the screen. He dragged his eyes away so that he could describe his first dream of the sandstorm. He told them about Sebastian making contact with him. He described his journey to the Sick Bay and meeting Michael.

"What was it like for you over the first two days in the Sick Bay, compared to what you were used to in the unit?" asked Jasper.

"It was a holiday but, more than that, it was like coming alive. It was like waking up from a long sleep. It took some time for the effects of the gas to wear off. At first, we sat on our own. Then we started to discover that we could chat together and how good that felt."

They showed some clips of Mark joining in the worship in the meeting.

"Tell us about how you feel about worship."

"I did not know it before, but I really love music. As soon as I heard worship, I was drawn. It touches me in a special way. It's hard to put in words. Sometimes the words strike a chord in my heart. Sometimes I just want to give myself completely to the Lord in the song. I love seeing other people responding - going deeper in worship."

He described the moment on the train that morning, when he opened the blind and saw the moors for the first time while Matt had played some moving music.

Jasper nodded showing he understood him well.

Jonathan addressed the three newcomers.

"Thank you so much for sharing. What is amazing to us is to see how much you have learnt in such a short space of time. It's been only a week! We have not seen the Lord do so much in new people like this. We believe there are some special things he has planned for you. We are excited that you are here. Imogen has a welcome present for you."

Imogen came up. She was beaming. Mark thought she radiated warmth and love. She handed each of them a screen device.

"These are for you, with our love. We have loaded the images of you when you were in the Nursery so many years ago, and some footage from the past week. They have the Bible, lots of music and teaching just like what you had to explore in the ward. You will have more to add in your time here. Yours to keep, with our love."

Everyone applauded and cheered as she gave each of them each a kiss and a hug. They could not conceal their pleasure. They waved to the crowd.

"And," she continued with a grin, "it's someone's birthday."

Rachel appeared, walking towards them with a large cake covered in little lights. Colour came into Johnson's cheeks. The crowd started singing 'Happy Birthday'. He seemed a little puzzled at the song but grinned.

"I can't remember having a cake before," said Johnson when they had done.

"We all used to sing that song on birthdays when we were kids like," said Rachel. "Now sweetheart, give a good blow on the candles." She demonstrated.

Johnson blew out the flames and there was a big cheer and more clapping. One candle spluttered back to life so he kept blowing on it. It refused to go out. He looked bewildered.

Amid the laughing, Rachel piped up.

"Don't worry, pet, it's a joke candle that 'un!"

Then Mark heard Jasper's voice call out.

"Is anyone ready to party?"

There were cheers all around. The crowd was ready to celebrate.

Jasper got behind the drums and started a foot-stomping beat. A man emerged with a bass guitar and the beat got stronger. Other players came forward with guitars, a keyboard, a fiddle and a squeezy bag with pipes sticking out. Imogen, Rachel and another woman grabbed the hands of the three newcomers and showed them some steps.

Mark glanced around. The meeting area was heaving with dancers. The young children threaded in and out through the grown-ups.

Mark was getting out of breath when the music changed and someone called out, "Dashing White Sergeant."

People arranged themselves in threes around the central area and a dance began. Mark was with Imogen and Johnson. They danced with another group of three, with each other, and then moved forward to join another threesome. They were surrounded by people turning in different directions.

At first Mark and Johnson were both lost but they were guided by Imogen and the other dancers. Because the music repeated, they soon began to understand the order and sequence of the dance.

Mark lost track of time and how many dances they did. He was amazed at the energy that the musicians had in their playing and the diversity of what they could play with such seeming effortlessness.

There was a break for some drinks.

He noticed the little boy with the blond curls being scooped by his father. The boy's head rested on the man's shoulder as he was carried away. It must be bedtime for that young one, Mark thought.

Johnson came by, filming as he went.

Another song was gathering tempo. Rachel took Mark's hand and led him back to the dance floor. He followed her steps as best he could.

At last, Jasper stood up and called out, "Let's finish with worship."

He began, one voice alone, "We will give God all our worship."

Without waiting, everyone joined in, "We will give him all our praise." They sang without any instruments. Mark marveled at the passion in their voices. He heard harmonies that added beauty and colour to the sound.

At the end, they said good night to more people than Mark could register. Jasper and Imogen gave each of them a warm hug.

They took their gifts in hand. Pete and Stevie walked with them back to the quarters. They were elated and weary.

"What an incredible day," said Johnson.

"I really like it up here," said Sanjay.

They all agreed.

Back in their quarters, Mark, Johnson and Sanjay washed and pulled on their pyjamas. They were grateful to lie down. They chatted for a while about the evening and the dancing and the people they had met.

Soon, with their eyes heavy, they fell asleep.

Late that night, Mark dreamt that he was a little boy. He played with his friends. He was without care or concern: a picture of inno-cence. A figure approached: it was his father. He scooped him up and Mark clung to him with two arms around his neck. He had a familiar smell. It felt very secure.

DAY 9

Mark awoke to an unfamiliar sound. At first, with sleep still clinging to him, he was unsure where he was. He listened in the dark room. There was a mixture of sounds. There were different combinations that repeated. For a while he tried to return to slumber, but it was too loud to ignore. Eventually, his curiosity brought him into consciousness, and he got up. The other two were still asleep so he pulled on his boots, grabbed his jacket, slipped out into the passage and made his way along it to the entrance. He went outside and blinked at the brightness of the daylight. Few people were up yet.

A path wandered into the wood and he followed it. As he neared trees and thick bushes, he spotted a flurry of quick movements in the shadows. It was the birds! They called out their song in turns. He strolled further, enjoying the sounds of the morning: the hustle of wind in the trees, the tapping of a woodpecker, and the faint tinkle of the stream with the constant chorus of bird song.

The path joined a track and he continued along it to a large bridge. He paused and peered down at the brown water below. The colour reminded him of tea, before you add milk.

He found a place where he could clamber down to the waterside. The stones were smooth in his hand and under his feet. The birds kept up their chorus in the trees above him. Some flitted across the stream so that he could make out their colours. He scooped up some water in his hands and tasted it. It was cold yet refreshing. It struck him that he could not remember what water tasted like in the city. How dull his senses had been, he thought. Here, he felt like his senses were sharper. The air had a certain quality; it was hard to put your finger on. It seemed so much more pure compared to the ventilated air they breathed in the city.

"Lord, this place is beautiful," he said.

Straightaway, a thought came into his mind, like it had been invisibly injected into his head.

"Everything I make is beautiful."

He made his way back to find the others, to wash and dress and, later, they had breakfast together.

Jasper came over and greeted them.

"Guys, we want to have a chance to talk this morning. Is there anything in particular you want to do later today, so we can see if we can fit it in?"

"Can we have a proper tour around the castle?" asked Sanjay.

Jasper smiled. "I hoped you would say that."

They went with him to the Communications Centre and into an inner room. Jonathan was waiting for them with Helena and Imogen. They greeted them and asked them to sit down. There were two large screens behind him and two of the Comms guys were working on screens beside him.

Jasper opened with a short introduction,

"Before we do anything, teach you anything, show you anything, there is something important we want to share. It's the big picture into which everything we do here fits."

Jonathan addressed them with a measure of seriousness:

"We want to give you an overview of how the world is, how it operates."

As he spoke, the two Comms guys flashed up images on the large screens to illustrate what he was saying.

"The whole world is under one government. The global economy is a total monopoly. The Executive own all resources on the earth and all peoples, the world over, are subject to them. They are like the kings of the earth. They rule the whole world.

"The world is organised into seven levels. You are Level Three Workers. The megacities were built to contain the Level Three Workers. The cities are based on the plan of the city quarter. There are one hundred Workers in a unit and one hundred units in a quarter - with dormitories and canteens and workspaces. There is no direct contact between the different cities for Level Three Workers. Each city is contained so that Workers do not have any knowledge of what happens outside their familiar surroundings, apart from what is fed to them through the screens. They do not understand the world, as it is, because it is not shown to them.

"Level Seven is the top level. Level Seven Executives and Level Six Leaders are at the top of the pyramid. They have their own communities, in the best locations the old world had to offer. They enjoy the best of everything: food, wine, homes, schools and possessions. They have some freedom to travel, within constraints based on security. They have some freedom to speak their minds.

"Level Five Maintainers live together in special bases and enjoy privileges like rest periods in specially built resorts. They are highly trained and carry weapons. Level Five Maintainers provide security for the whole system. They step in if there is any trouble or if there is a rebellion. Their units can react at very short notice. They are ruthless and kill if they are ordered to kill.

"Level Four Supervisors live in separate sectors around the megacities. They have separate facilities and some privileges. Level Three Workers do not own anything and do not travel from their cities except to the resorts outlying their cities, if they are loyal and are chosen in the Lottery. The Workers who are in transport, stay in separate communities so that they do not share their knowledge of the world with Level Three Workers in the cities.

"Level Two Workers farm the land and fish in the seas and work in processing factories outside the cities. They are contained in their communes. They produce food and resources for all the other Levels. They do not travel to the cities. Many of them did not qualify as Level Three Workers because they were uneducated, or unfit, or they were in families where knowledge of working the land and the sea was passed down from generation to generation.

"Level One are Refusers and Incapables. The Refusers are prisoners. They are at the bottom of the pile. They work long hours of hard labour in mines and quarries. They live in work camps. They receive basic provisions. They do not get any rest periods like Level Two and Level Three do. They are generally treated harshly. The Incapables are the ones who are too old or are unfit to serve. The old people from Levels Two to Five are kept in separate retirement settlements."

Jonathan paused to check their faces and see if they were taking this in.

"Who are the Refusers? Why are they prisoners?" asked Sanjay.

Mark thought for a moment how, not long ago, he would have been taken aback if someone his age had asked a question so freely and directly.

Jonathan continued.

"The Refusers are the ones who would not accept the New Order. The Executive could have terminated all of them, but they decided to put them to work against their will, to contribute to the Common Good. They reasoned that they might even accept the New Order and then they might agree to work in Level Two. Level Ones are considered as so dangerous that they are watched over by armed guards with dogs. They are kept in fenced camps with very basic living conditions. People who refused to bow the knee to the New Order because of their faith and beliefs were made Level One Refusers."

"Do you know any Level One people?" asked Johnson.

Jonathan glanced towards Jasper and Imogen.

"Our dad is a Level One," said Imogen, slowly. "He was a teacher and a writer: a believer. He spoke out against the New Order when the war began. After the war, they tested him and decided he was too much of a risk. We believe he was taken to Siberia, in Russia. We are not sure because we have not been able to track some Level Ones yet."

Mark searched for bitterness in Imogen's face but did not find any. She blinked and a single tear traced down her cheek.

"Do you want to go and break him out?" asked Sanjay. His fist was clenched.

"Only if God directs us. I believe God is using him, wherever he is. We pray for him often." Jasper's voice was calm.

"What about your mother?" asked Johnson.

"She died in the war," answered Jasper solemnly.

They realised that their questions were prying and they went quiet.

Jonathan continued.

"The way the New Order worked on you was to keep you placid. They do not want you to think for yourself. Your questions show me that you are already thinking for yourselves. It was not like this two weeks ago. From an early age you were taught not to ask questions. They trained you not to make decisions for yourself but to rely completely on the system for all your needs: food; clothes; a place to sleep, to wash and work. All your needs are met by the system so the New Order is your father, your protector, and your god. It is ingrained in every Worker from childhood. You did not know any different. You were coached to have faith in the New Order to provide you with everything you need. You did not have any alternative, except to be removed as a Refuser. You were forbidden to question the system. You would be a threat if you did. They know that ideas can spread like a virus. That is why every unit is contained within its own block. The block design is repeated through the city. The city is segregated into male and female sectors. The day you went to the Hospital Complex was the first time you had been out of the block for over two years - when you were transferred from the School Complex.

"In the old world, we made our own decisions. We could decide what to wear, what to eat, what to think and what to say. We had freedom of movement, for the most part. We lived where we could find work and where we wanted to live or could afford, with the money we had. You could own property. Money was the currency for buying things. We earned money in our jobs and we spent money in many ways, as we needed. We bought a house, we had a car, and we had lots of things in our house. We bought clothes, food - everything we needed. People would spend a lot of their time talking to each other. Friendships were one of the things that made life worth living: knowing others and being known by other people.

"The New Order is set up on a completely different basis. It says that your life has worth because you obey the rules for the Common Good, which you learnt as children. You are trained not to challenge the system. If you questioned the system, you might not agree to follow instructions every hour of every day."

The more the older man spoke, the more Mark's head was filled with questions.

"What happened in the war?" he asked.

Jonathan looked at him then nodded at the Comms guys before continuing.

"The war was very carefully planned. It was a global coup, organised by the majority of the world's elite. Most of them were already in government and in positions of authority. Many of the leaders were already meeting in secret, long before the war. They had to eliminate all the leaders who refused to join them. If you were a leader, either you were in or you were out.

"They engineered a cocktail of disastrous events: financial meltdown in well developed countries, famine in poor countries in Africa, disease in parts of Asia, an epidemic in Europe and America, a religious war in the Middle East, fears of a global environmental catastrophe that were inflated. They all coincided so that the whole world was affected. Every country faced crisis. They manipulated people in all countries, rich and poor, into thinking that the New Order was the solution. They pushed all the nations into a global crisis. The world was desperate; right on the edge. They presented a way out and people bought into it. They promised jobs for everyone, they promised a bright future but they did not give them the truth. They did not tell them that they would be divided or that many would be sedated."

"Did people fight back?" asked Johnson.

"Yes," replied Jonathan. "In many countries, people took up arms to resist them. It took about four months to quell all the resistance. They waited for people to muster in groups in remote areas, then they made air strikes and missile attacks - wiped them out. Sometimes they sent in people to talk peace and then the bombs would fall. There were some places where the resistance was strong and the fighting was fierce, like in the Swiss mountains and the Southern plains of America. One of the last places to fall was Afghanistan because the Afghans had been fighting outsiders for more than four generations.

Mark looked at the images of determined faces, bronzed by years of sun.

"Why was religion taken away?" asked Mark. "Could they not give believers a country somewhere?"

Jonathan smiled at the question and shook his head.

"For many of the peoples of the earth, faith was the foundation of their freedom and their independence. That sense of freedom had to be completely removed for the New Order to dominate and to control the world. Their goal was one world government and they would not tolerate even one country where people had liberty. Faith was an enemy, a potent threat, so it was outlawed. All references to faith in the megacities were deleted. For Christians, meeting had to be in secret. The church was driven underground."

"You said you fled to a remote place in Scotland," said Johnson.

"That's right. We went to a cottage near a place called Rannoch. It was well off the beaten track. It was a place where outlaws used to hide out centuries ago. We stayed there while the war was fought.

"When victory was declared, everyone was called upon to apply for positions in cities, on farms and communes. That was when God showed us that we should come up here and apply to work here. They needed people. We found Jasper and we took to meeting and praying for the camp. We had a house in a village nearby and one day, a family came to join us. It has slowly grown over the years. We get people from the cities who need a refreshing and teaching."

"Why don't you go and invade the cities?" asked Sanjay.

"We exist to serve the Lord," replied Helena this time. "He is sovereign, he is our king and our leader. Our job is to listen to the Spirit and follow as best we can. He has told us to not fight a human fight. We war, but we war in the spirit, through prayer. We are subversive. Yes, we long for the Lord to come and unravel the whole system and set all the captives free. But if we went on our own strength and our own will, we would certainly fail. We would be found and probably sent to a Level One camp or simply killed."

"Look at you," said Jonathan, gesturing towards them. "Would you be here if Sebastian had not been faithful and courageous enough to make contact with you, without being caught? He had our support, both physical and spiritual.

We pray for the Lord to add to our number all the time."

"That is what John said," added Johnson. "Why does someone like Sebastian come here and then go back to the city when he could stay here?"

Jonathan nodded. It was a fair question.

"We prayed with him. The Lord told him very clearly that he wanted him back in the city. To obey is better than sacrifice. It is better to give than to receive. Sebastian has great joy because of you guys crossing over and moving deeper into faith. It makes his sacrifice worthwhile. He knows the Lord is pleased with him. The Lord loves radical obedience. He is looking for people with hearts fully committed to him. Apart from our faith, nothing matters. We are here for him. Death does not frighten us."

"We are sending updates to the church in New Birmingham so they hear our news," added Jasper, "and we can organise to make a group call to the church."

"How did you hack into the system to get us to the hospital ward and then onto the train safely?" asked Mark, still curious.

"We have some of the best Comms guys and they are working in different countries. Some are under cover, but they work together. Through prayer, they had insights into how they could manipulate the system. It means we can move people without it being alerted."

"Why did they do it – the leaders of the war, the people who planned the coup and took over?" asked Sanjay. He spoke slowly; his voice was serious.

"That is a good question." Jonathan rubbed his chin before answering.

"The heart of man is naturally set against God's ways. The first man, Adam, went astray and his sin affects everyone so that they have to come to Jesus and accept him as Saviour and Lord then they are forgiven. They are then able to live for God and not for another. People who do not yield to the Lord have a tendency towards control. You can see it through many periods of history: empire after empire built by warring leaders, seeking to lord it over many peoples. Those people who have significant power tend to yearn for absolute power. The leaders of the New Order were seduced by what they thought they could achieve. They were motivated by greed, pride, and control. They used lies, deception, fear and force to reach their goal. They knew that many countries of the world would not adopt the system willingly so they had to resort to half truths, falsities, deceit, manipulation and, ultimately, force. They were unaware that they were collaborating with the Enemy, the one who hates everything God has made, the one who opposes everything the Lord has planned. The Lord came to set us free. The Enemy comes to make us captives, to keep us from experiencing liberty."

Jonathan paused. The three newcomers were pensive, considering what he had said.

"I think we should break for coffee," suggested Jasper.

"The school group is coming in ten," said one of the Comms guys.

They walked over towards the castle. Jonathan and Helena went to stand near the drawbridge while they stayed back by the trees. They watched while the drone transporter landed on the grass and a group of teenage boys in uniform with two teachers got out and went over to be greeted by Jonathan and Helena. The group headed in to the castle to be shown around.

"This happens from time to time," said Jasper. "Schools do tours of the area. They will be gone in about an hour."

For the rest of the morning they stayed in the Comms room, exploring archive material from the time of the war and the early years of the New World Order.

They went back to the castle dining room for lunch and Stevie and Pete came to join them. They chatted throughout about the war and how things were before the war.

"You said you wanted a tour," said Jasper, when they had cleared the table.

He and Imogen led Sanjay, Johnson and Mark back outside, via the front door.

Jasper pointed out the coat of arms on the wall above the front door and explained to them what it signified: the marriage of a Campbell man and a Stuart woman, with the date 1672.

Inside, they climbed up a level to the room at the base of the tower. The light was dim from two narrow arrow slits in the East wall. There was an ancient tree in the centre of the stone vaulted room. The trunk was slender and blackened with age. Jasper told them about a family legend: a distant ancestor had had a dream. He was instructed by an angel. He should gather his treasure, load it onto his donkey then let his laden donkey wander, and follow it at a discrete distance. Where it sat down to rest in the evening, he should build his castle, and his family would prosper. The man followed the instructions and that evening the donkey sat under one of three trees to rest.

"Is this the actual tree?" blurted out Sanjay, touching the trunk.

"Yes," Imogen replied, "it is a holly tree. I think it's remarkable that they did not toss it on the fire on a cold night. Years ago, our grandfather cut off a piece and sent it to London to be dated. They came back with a date: 1370. Our grandfather was the 24th Thane. The man who started building the castle was the 3rd Thane."

"What is a thane?" asked Mark.

"When Scotland was ruled by a king, he had a group of knights to support him. Our family was entrusted to protect this area around Nairn for the king. When the king went to battle, the thanes were expected to show up with soldiers to make up the army." Jasper lent back on the ancient stonework.

"But why are the walls are so thick?" asked Sanjay. He was over by the window. He could see that the outside walls were over a metre and a half thick from the depth of the recess.

"In those days, the Scots were often at war with each other. There were separate groups called clans. Often a clan would have a long-standing conflict with another clan. They called it a feud. Sometimes there were invasions from armies from other countries. You would generally not be safe in a timber house. Castles were built in stone all over Europe from the 12th century onwards."

"How do you know all of this?" asked Sanjay.

"Some we learnt from our father when we were children, we learnt about castles at school, some I studied when I was older and some I have researched here," answered Jasper. "About five years ago, we had a massive breakthrough after some of our Comms guys prayed for a way to secretly access the Archive of the New Order and the Lord showed them a way in."

He led them up the tower and showed them the large rooms on the three floors above. The floors were connected by a tight, spiral staircase cut in stone, that was dimly lit by narrow arrow slits. Mark was amazed to see how the stone treads had been worn over generations: he was stepping where men and women of the 14th century had stepped.

A narrow flight at the top led up to small door. Jasper pulled and it swung inwards so that they could climb out onto the battlements, blinking in the bright daylight after the gloom inside. On the West side, there was the small river that Mark recognised from his morning ramble. They could see the blue bridge. The tallest trees had high branches up at their level. A light breeze ruffled their hair. They peered down to the courtyard below. From the East side they could see the layout of some of the camp from up here. A mixture of sounds reached their ears: gardeners working; children calling; hammering in the workshop. A pigeon swung past, heading to the wood. To the North, they could see the sea in the distance. Shadows from the clouds were moving across the fields towards the North East.

"Was this castle famous?" asked Johnson.

Jasper looked at Imogen and she answered.

"Before the war, this place was well known because it was mentioned in a play by a famous writer called William Shakespeare. He wrote a series of plays between about 1590 and 1610. He was world famous - he was regarded as one of the best writers in the English language. Dad told us that he thought Shakespeare must have come here because some of the detail in the play could have only been written by someone who had come to this area and who knew this place. The king he wrote the play for was a Scot, a Stuart, and the first king to rule all of Wales, England and Scotland together. His name was James. He was the one to bring in a flag to represent England and Scotland. It was called the Union Jack. His nephew, also a Stuart, lived a few miles over there to the East."

She pointed in that direction.

"Shakespeare could have joined the king on a tour of this area. It would not have been safe for a Londoner like him to come up here alone, in those days. He could easily have been robbed and killed. Our ancestors did not go anywhere unless they were armed. They even used to keep a small dagger in their sock."

Imogen stared into the distance, towards the North and the sea.

"We used to live in London when we were children. You could go to the theatre and watch a Shakespeare play or many other shows. London was a vibrant city in those days: full of people from numerous countries. It was one of the great cities of the world. I remember our dad took us to see the Olympic Games when they came to London in 2012. I was almost twelve."

"Olympic Games, did you say?" asked Johnson.

"Yes," answered Jasper. "Every four years, there was a huge contest with all sorts of events. About two hundred countries sent men and women to compete. If you came third in your event, you won a bronze medal, second got a silver medal and the winner was given a gold medal. Here at camp, we try to keep alive all the games we learnt before the War. That is one of the reasons we play football."

Imogen led them back down to the first floor and along a long corridor, showing them bedrooms with ornate beds. She told them about the 14th Thane: a woman called Muriel Calder. She was born in about 1498. When she was young, she was branded, like a cow, because her uncles feared that she would be taken because she was the heir to the title. When she was ten or eleven, she was kidnapped by the Campbell's. She was taken to their castle on the West side of Scotland. She was married off to the youngest son of the chief when she was old enough. She lived until she was seventy.

"Dad lived here from the age of five. He used to sprint down this corridor to bed at night."

The three looked at her, puzzled.

"At night, when it was dark, all these doorways were in shadow. He imagined that baddies might be waiting to kidnap him. If he ran fast enough, they might not catch him!"

They grinned.

The main bedroom was hung with tapestries. They had scenes from the Bible, like Moses leading the people of Israel across the Red Sea. The three had never seen biblical depictions before and they studied them closely, finding Moses with a long beard and trying to work out which one, among the other figures, was his brother, Aaron.

The bed was a four-poster with feathers at the top of each of the posts.

"Dad told us that when he was little, occasionally when there was thunder and lightning at night, if he was scared and could not sleep, he would creep in and sleep between his mother and father. He felt so safe, snuggled up between them," Imogen smiled as she spoke.

"He grew up here as a child and now he is a prisoner of the New Order?"

Johnson spoke with incredulity.

"That's right. When the New Order was imposed, some people were left with almost nothing," Jasper said. "A few were winners, most were losers. You could say that many were prisoners of the New Order, on many of the Levels."

They showed them the bedroom wings and where the servants used to sleep in the attics. Some of the attics were packed with things from before the war. They had a rummage in some old wardrobes so that they could show them old kilts and clothes from generations ago.

Later on, they descended to the basement down more stone steps. Imogen opened an old wooden door and flicked a light switch. There was a long vaulted room, painted white, with a table along its length. There was an assortment of old kitchen equipment.

"This was the kitchen from the 17th century until grandfather was a young boy in the early 1930's."

She showed them the fresh water well and explained that it was an essential resource whenever the castle was under siege.

She then led them through what would have been dungeons and stables.

"When we were young, the castle was open to the public. This area was the gift shop." Under dust covers there were still shelves with a range of gifts and baskets of toys that they delved into, picking up small toys, woollen gloves and tartan scarves. In one window, there was a display of knives. There was so much to look at but eventually Jasper and Imogen suggested they go for tea.

They slipped up some back stairs and emerged near the entrance. They went into a small dining room where hot teapots and warm scones where waiting for them.

Johnson wanted to know what it was like living in London when they were children. Jasper explained that they could get about on buses and trains but there was sometimes the threat of being mugged, if they were alone. Imogen told them about the shopping you could do. They explained how everyone used money to pay for things. Mark was amazed to hear about how people owned their own things, even when they were children. Imogen said that many people would get caught up in accumulating more and more possessions.

They cleared tea and went out into the afternoon sunshine. They walked across the blue bridge, along the village street to the school. They met many of the children. Mark greeted the boy with the blonde curls. Imogen wanted to show them the Art room.

"Come and see their work," she said with a broad grin.

She asked some of the children to come with them.

She showed them numerous drawings and paintings.

"They were working on two themes," she explained, "one was 'What is God like', the other was 'Blessing: what it means to me'."

"Who is their teacher?" asked Johnson.

"I am," she answered with a contented smile.

Later that afternoon, Jasper and Imogen showed them the camp gardens. They met some of the garden team. Two of the team, dressed in grubby overalls, showed them some of the green-houses and growing tunnels. Mark noticed their boots caked in mud and dirt under their finger-nails. Their hands were lined. They showed them how they nursed seedlings to young plants and invited them to join them moving the seedlings to larger pots.

Mark had never felt soil in his fingers before. The feel of it touched him deeply in his soul in a way he could not express.

He was delighted at the sight of so many young vegetables growing: it was a wonder. When they showed them the seed stores and he felt how light those little generators of life were, it seemed almost incredible.

"How can something so small produce a new plant?" he asked with wide eyes.

"It is amazing isn't it," said one of the gardeners, "from one seed comes the whole plant and, when it is ready, many more seeds. I love to ponder the work of the Creator God in here. He provides the means of multiplication."

They entered a large greenhouse divided into sections with large, circular containers as high as their shoulders, and full of tall plants and flowers. When they looked at the water in the containers, it seemed like it was frothing.

A woman with bright eyes explained that this was where they treated the wastewater from the camp. She took a clear tube and showed them the small creatures that were busy consuming the bacteria in the water. At the end of the lines of containers, there was a pond with fish swimming in it. She showed them how the water was ready to be used in the gardens or on the farm.

"How clever it is that God has given us ways to take something dirty and make it clean with little creatures he has provided," remarked the woman. "We are learning to appreciate every creature he has given to the world."

They headed back to the camp as the late afternoon light was beginning to fade. The evening game of football was well underway. They joined in with enthusiasm. Mark loved the feeling of running and he understood more of the different positions people were holding: the game could not flow if players crowded around the ball.

After the game, they went and showered and changed before supper. Pete and Stevie walked with them to the canteen. They discussed what they had seen that day.

"Did yous see any ghosts?" asked Rachel.

"Ghosts?" asked Johnson.

"She is messing with you," said Imogen. "Over the years, people said they saw ghosts there but not me."

The meeting was ready to start.

Most of the camp had gathered, including the older children.

Helena and Jonathan welcomed everyone and then led a quiet time for prayer. They asked a small group to join them.

"The Intercessors have been deep in prayer today so we asked them to come and share," said Helena.

A noble, older lady stepped forward and spoke. Mark thought she must have been well educated because there was an easy eloquence in her words.

"Dear people, three days ago, the Lord started laying on us a burden to pray for the lost. We waited for him to direct us. We found ourselves praying for those people who were wounded during the war and those who have been treated harshly by the New Order. We repented on behalf of the leaders who were brutal, careless and cruel. They sinned against heaven and against people on earth. The Lord led us to pray for many parts of the world. We believe that he is going to focus our prayer on one particular country over the next few days. We believe that he may call us out to go to that country and bring hope to the hopeless, to speak healing to the wounded, and to proclaim freedom to the prisoners. I believe that he will put a burden to pray on many of us, because we are one body and we share his burden; a burden that is light because Jesus is interceding in heaven."

"Let's go into worship and see where he leads us," said Jonathan.

Jasper and Imogen led worship for several songs. Mark thought that there was a lovely understanding between them and with the other musicians and singers. There was a song with words of deep crying out to deep and then a song about power, waiting as one, and the burning in souls. Passion was rising in the whole gathering.

Mark spotted the little boy with the blonde curls and two other children go right up and whisper in Jonathan's ear. While the music gently continued in the background, Jonathan indicated for them to share.

Mark was touched to hear their young voices.

"While we were worshipping, we saw angels coming up and standing with us. They are big and strong." They pointed to places in the area. "There are many more in a ring around us, standing guard. They shine brighter when we sing from our hearts."

Jasper started a steady beat on the drums. "Holy, holy, holy is the Lord God Almighty," sang Imogen.

There was a swell of response from the gathering. People called out, some began speaking in tongues; some made a sound like a loud wail. There seemed to Mark to be a gust of wind that went through the space. Some people went down on the floor, some knelt. Many of the children were dancing by the singers. Mark raised his hands as high as they would go and sang with all his might.

The next song was about going where God called. Everyone including the children seemed to join with one voice, like there was agreement in every heart. Mark found himself offering himself to the Lord wholeheartedly, without any reservation.

The music became more down tempo and the songs more personal. There was a period of quiet when some people called out words of prophecy and prayers. The focus shifted to prayers asking the Lord to call more people into his kingdom. Most people were kneeling and some were even crying as they prayed.

Mark opened his eyes to see Johnson and Sanjay were ready to head back. The meeting continued while many drifted away, as it was getting late. The three joined Pete and they walked back to the sleeping quarters.

"How long will the meeting go on for?" asked Mark.

"Well," replied Pete, "it might go on very late. There have been times when a meeting will go on until dawn. Sometimes the Intercessors pray non-stop, taking it in turns, so that there is constant prayer."

The three were grateful to get into their beds, after a long day.

That night Mark dreamt he was standing in front of a large crowd. They were all looking towards him with expectation. He knew that the Lord was close, helping him, so that he was not afraid. He felt tremendous excitement.

DAY 10

At breakfast the next morning, Jasper joined them.

"We have a few things we need to do today," he told them. "We should take you over to the farm. We need you to spend some hours working on the farm so that we can capture some footage on the cameras that we can feed into the system for observation if we need to. There are only a few cameras on the farm. You might find you enjoy it."

He took them over to a large board.

"We put our names here to volunteer to help in different parts of the camp. If we spend the morning on the farm, what would you like to do this afternoon?" he asked.

Johnson put his name down for Construction and Sanjay added his name to the Kitchen team. Mark thought for a moment. He remembered the feel of the soil yesterday and opted for the Garden team. He turned back to Jasper.

"I would love to have a go at getting involved in music somehow," he said.

"I was hoping you would say that," answered Jasper with a wide smile. "How about we go for our first jam after the afternoon session?"

"Jam? What is a jam?" Mark asked, puzzled.

"Oh, a jam is when we play around and practice," laughed Jasper. "Now guys, let's go to the garages, I want to show you something."

They made their way back to the yard, close to where the lorry had parked on their arrival. People smiled and greeted them as they passed. Jasper led them into a shed with lines of strange contractions. He pulled one forward.

"This is a bicycle. We have adapted it to make it easy for first-timers like you."

He showed them how to sit, how to pedal, how to steer and how to brake. He pointed to the stabilizer wheels at the rear.

"Watch how these help me to get going. They lift up and fold away when I am moving faster, because the bike is more stable when it is moving. Keep your feet on the pedals and your hands here, on the handlebars."

He demonstrated for them in the yard. Back in the shed, he showed them a machine like a mounted gym bike, and gave them each a try so that they could get the feel of pedaling and braking.

He handed them protective gear.

"Just in case you lose control," he paused and grinned, "we don't want you to crash and burn."

Then he pulled out a bike each and encouraged them to follow him out of the yard. They started slowly and unsteadily because the action seemed very strange to them, but soon they were delighted to be moving along a track past fields and a wood. The feeling was like nothing Mark had felt before. The sun was strengthening so that the landscape looked fresh, bursting with life. They hooted and called to each other as they pedaled. Jasper surprised them when he suddenly stopped, kicking up his rear wheel, and then went forward and pulled a wheelie. They called out their approval.

They approached the farm buildings. They came to a stop in the farmyard and stowed the bikes. Jasper led them into the farm office and explained where the cameras were, before they put on overalls and wellie boots. He showed them the cowshed. They helped him move the cows to another section so that they could clean out the floor of the shed and put down fresh straw.

Stevie drove up in an enormous tractor and leapt out. They went inside for a tea break.

Jasper and Stevie answered their questions about the farm and the local area. They were joined by some more of the team.

The three visitors wanted to see what crops they grew so Jasper and Stevie led them over to a vehicle. Mark read its name at the front: Land Rover. They climbed aboard and they toured the farm with Jasper at the wheel. The farm stretched for several miles along the river and up onto a series of ridges to the South. They bumped down some muddy tracks and stopped several times to show them the young crops and how the soil changed on different parts of the farm.

It was time for lunch so they stopped and sat on the car bonnet and ate the sandwiches they had brought.

They headed back to the farm and then took the bikes back to the camp. They parted to join their teams. Johnson went to help the Construction team extend the men's sleeping quarters. Sanjay headed for the kitchens to help make dinner and Mark walked down to the gardens.

He was greeted by the two gardeners he had met the day before. They were called Paul and Becky. They gave him some overalls and they prepared trays with soil and compost. Paul brought out seeds for them to plant. Becky explained how they would encourage germination and what temperature and humidity the plants would flourish in.

Later, they went along the rows of young plants in one greenhouse checking the delicate sprinkler heads that would deliver the correct moisture at regular intervals.

They were having a break when Pete arrived.

"Jonathan has asked if you would like to come and be prayed for."

"You should go," said Paul. "We call Jonathan "Heaven's Doorman," because people often meet God in a special way when he prays for them."

"And Helena might be there too," added Becky.

Mark went with Pete to the castle. Jonathan and Helena were waiting for them in a room in the tower, on the first floor and greeted him.

Jonathan explained what they would like to do.

"Imagine your bloodline is like a pipe. It flows through you from your ancestors. God wants the blood to be clean but the Enemy wants it polluted. People often need cleaning up if things have come on their spiritual blood-line, or if something difficult has happened in their life. We will ask the Spirit to lead you. We will ask the questions and wait for you to receive the revelation. The Lord will have something he wants to shine a light on today."

He asked Mark if he was ready and he nodded in response. Mark sat in a chair and closed his eyes. The room fell silent.

Jonathan began by declaring the goodness of God over Mark, then asking the Lord to give Mark eyes to see, ears to hear and the ability to sense what the Spirit was saying. He went on to ask the Lord to show what he wanted to set Mark free of today.

"What do you sense, Mark?" he asked.

Mark said he had a picture of a man sitting at a desk. Jonathan asked the Lord to show Mark whether the man was an ancestor on his mother's side or on his father's side.

"Father's side," said Mark. He had a picture of his father in his mind.

Jonathan asked the Lord to show him how many generations back the man was.

"I see a board with the number five on it," Mark replied.

Jonathan asked the Lord to show him clearly what situation the man in the picture was in.

"He is in despair, like things are hopeless, as if he is abandoned."

Jonathan asked the Lord to show Mark what had come on the bloodline through the man's despair. As Mark called out a list of several things, Jonathan wrote them down, then he led Mark though a process of forgiving his ancestor and cutting off the sin that had come down the bloodline as a result.

Jonathan asked the Lord to show Mark the result of what he had prayed.

Mark gave him a commentary on what he could see.

"I can see the cross. I am standing in front of it, looking up at it. It's like a hidden door that is now opening. I am stepping through the opening. I am in a dark space, but there is a shaft of light coming down from heaven. I am stepping out of the shadows into the shaft of light. Now I am standing in the light. I am rising very fast. The Father is drawing me up into his presence. I am up in the clouds. I am strong and yet I am light. I can move easily. I have so much energy, I feel like I will never get tired. Now the Lord is showing me that I am a weapon. I am like a long spear, like a missile in His hand. He aims me at part of the earth far below and I shoot down at incredible speed and hit the mark. I hit the ground but I don't even feel a thing. The impact, when I hit the ground, has split the earth - there's a big crack, like after an earthquake. The ground seems very dry with hardly any sign of anything green; it is desolate. God is going to achieve something from the cracking, where I hit the ground."

"Well done," said Jonathan, "you see clearly. That was your spirit man you saw. You saw heaven. You have hope and faith now. You have confidence to go through the gate."

"How do you feel now?" asked Helena.

"I feel like a weight has been lifted off. It's a kind of relief, like I don't have to worry anymore. That was a fabulous thing, being up in heaven like that," answered Mark with a big smile.

Jonathan and Helena then prayed prayers of blessing over Mark.

He felt like he was wrapped in light and love when they prayed.

Later on, when they joined the others at supper, Sanjay and Johnson gazed at Mark as if they had noticed something.

"You look different," ventured Sanjay. The others looked up.

"I feel different," replied Mark. "I feel like I was carrying a weight around and it has dropped off." He paused. "I had lots of fears - like I was constantly afraid that we were going to be caught or something bad was going to happen. I feel like many fears have gone."

"Your face is different," said Imogen slowly, looking at him intently. "Before, you had a shadow in your eyes: a look like you were hunted. Your eyes have more light in them now."

Mark smiled at her and told them about his experience of being lifted up to heaven.

"Did you see the Father?" asked Johnson.

"Not really. He was there, he was near, but it was like I had a glimpse. I was near his shoulder. I was tiny compared to him. I am not sure I could have looked at him and survived." Mark pondered this for a moment.

"How did you step through the cross?" asked Sanjay.

"It was like it had hinges. I was looking at it, and then it opened. It swung open like a big door. What had been background behind the cross was like a picture on part of the door. The door opened and there was a dark space behind. It's hard to explain."

"The shaft of light you mentioned. How big was it?" asked Jasper.

"It was big enough for me to step into and be surrounded by light," responded Mark. "Was that normal?"

Helena spoke next. Mark felt the care in her voice and in her eyes.

"Everyone has an experience that means something special to them. Time and again, we have seen the Lord reveal things to a person that speak deeply to their soul. He knows us better than we know ourselves. Remember how we began by asking the Lord to show what he wanted to set you free from? We give him an open invitation. He does not work in formulas. He is creative. He is wise. He knows what we need. His timing is not just pretty good, it's perfect."

"I want to give you a hug," said Imogen and she went over to him and wrapped him in her arms. Mark received her embrace. His heart was touched as she held him.

Jonathan asked Sanjay and Johnson to come for prayer before the evening meeting.

"Mark, do you want to come with us while

we warm up for the worship tonight?" asked Jasper, as Mark watched the other two go.

Mark nodded and they walked together to the meeting place.

Jasper showed him a keyboard that had been set up for him. The keys were coloured to identify the different notes.

"This screen will guide you in what to play," he explained. "We have set it up to show colours so that you can play along, with some harmonies. We will set it for each song. We usually don't know in advance exactly which songs we are going to play."

The other band members arrived and they played some songs together. Mark followed as best he could.

Soon people were filling the area and it was time to open the meeting.

After Jonathan had welcomed everyone, he said, "let's say the Lord's prayer together."

They followed the words on the screens but when they got to the words *your kingdom come*, they repeated it three times, with passion.

Jonathan nodded to Jasper as the signal to begin the music for worship.

"Mark, you choose the first song," said Jasper.

Mark felt everyone looking his way.

He closed his eyes and prayed silently, "What should I say?"

The thought came like an arrow, *What does your heart say?*

"Please can we sing *The Cross*," he replied, "and can we sing it out to the people who do not yet know who Jesus is and what he has done; people like my parents and the guys back in my unit."

It was a song he had found in the Sick Bay. Everyone seemed to give him a smile and a nod.

One of the band started on a keyboard. The words came up on the screen and everyone joined with Mark, as Jasper played the beat on the drums. Mark played some of the bass line on his keyboard. The voices swelled with the words, "When will you see that he died for you?"

Imogen came up to join the band and pressed Mark's shoulder as she passed him.

As Mark watched, he could see there was such oneness between Jasper and Imogen, as they led the assembly in the next songs. They only had to look at each other and they would know who was leading into the next song.

Imogen looked over to Mark then she spoke to the woman on one the guitars and she started to sing another song, "Who is there that loves me as I am, not demanding more than I can be?"

Mark remembered the song from one of the first meetings in the church back in the city.

Imogen sang like a child to their parent,

"He is God, He is good, He's my Father…"

Mark turned his gaze to see how people were responding. Some were kneeling; many had their hands up high. It was beautiful.

"Who is there that wipes my tears away?" sang Imogen. "Giving me the strength to face today."

He could feel the Spirit touching him, his chest around his heart felt sort of numb and tingly.

The noble looking lady, who spoke the night before, came forward as the song ended, with some of the other Intercessors.

"It is time to ask the Lord which nation he is going to send us to. Join me as I pray… Father, we ask you now to reveal what is in your heart. Which nation will you send us to?"

There was some din as different sounds combined: there were some people wailing, some calling out in tongues, and some calling out to the Lord.

After some minutes, the noble lady addressed the gathering again.

"I believe God is saying to us, it's Iceland."

There was a swell of response as many called out in agreement and many others just made a loud noise of approval.

"Let's continue to worship and then we will ask for direction and detail later," added the lady. She and the Intercessors withdrew.

Imogen closed her eyes, Jasper watched her intently. The din subsided and then she started to sing a song Mark did not recognise. Her voice was slow and gentle, like a mother to a child.

"Soften my heart, so I can know your love for me."

As the words came up, the rest of the band and the voices of the gathered people joined her, "Enter in, come to rule and reign, as I worship you this day."

Mark sang with them and played some notes on his keyboard. He caught sight of Sanjay and Johnson in the crowd. They had arms raised high, like most of the rest of the group, including the children. The song built to a gradual crescendo with the words, "I am yours, and you are mine."

Mark felt something pass him, like a breath of air and looked around. The Holy Spirit was moving through the throng. Some people were keeling over, some were shaking on the spot, and some were laughing like drunkards. There was a clang near him, as one woman on guitar hit the deck and shook. Some of the children were hopping up and down like pogo sticks. Mark saw Jasper struggling to stay on his stool as the shaking hit him. Imogen was doubled up, her arms moving like pistons: it was comical. He was about to laugh when something like an invisible fist hit him on the breast and sent him backwards onto the floor. He lay there quaking and flailing. He felt like hands had reached into his body and were jerking his insides up and down. He wanted to laugh but his teeth were chattering. His arms seemed to be moving like a crazy conductor and now he could not hold in the laughter. It came up from deep down and erupted loudly. He could hear that there were many others affected with similar merriment. It seemed to move around the meeting like ripples, round and round, wave after wave. The few people still standing were bent over with their heads pressed down towards the floor, as they let out loud groans. The meeting looked like a mad house.

"What would my Unit Supervisors think of this?" thought Mark and another wave of laughter rose up within him.

Eventually the meeting calmed down and people bid each other good night. Mark, Sanjay and Johnson headed back with Pete and Stevie. Sanjay was limping. He said that he had felt like bolts of electricity were making his body shudder. Johnson said it was like someone had gripped his body and had turned him into a rattle. They all felt tired but elated. They were ready to fall into bed and see what tomorrow would bring.

They did not realise it yet, but God had worked into them peace and readiness to respond to his call for this next chapter. They slept like young children, feeling safe and content.

That night Mark dreamed of happy days during his childhood in the Nursery, watched over by Imogen and the other nurses.

DAY 11

The next morning, there was a buzz about the camp. They went to breakfast. Everyone was talking about the mission to Iceland. The three quizzed the others on what they knew about the country. No one in the camp had been there before, explained Pete. The word was there would be a morning meeting at nine-thirty.

Jasper came over to them with two men who looked different. He introduced the visitors.

"Franz and Joseph have just arrived from Germany."

They stood and shook hands.

"Have you been here before?" asked Johnson.

"No, this is our first time," replied Franz. "We are part of the church in New Hamburg. The Lord spoke to us yesterday and told us to come here. He said he is going to do something special and he wants us to be part of it."

"We have many friends over there," said Jasper. "For years, when my dad was young, the British and the Germans did not co-operate much, hindered with the memories of two ugly world wars. We have found that the Lord loves it when we move together in unity. It's exciting that you guys are here. Come and meet the other leaders."

He led them away with a friendly wave to go and meet Jonathan, Helena and Imogen.

"The meeting this morning is gonnay to be a good one, I can feel it," said Stevie. He shook his clenched hands to express his excitement.

"Word is already getting around," said Pete, nodding towards different groups that were talking animatedly.

Before nine-thirty, the meeting area was filled up with the whole community. On the screens, the Comms guys played live messages from some of the other European churches. Mark was glad when he recognised John speaking from New Birmingham. John said that they were arranging prayer support from their whole group and were sending provisions and equipment on another train due to meet them over in Iceland.

Jasper stood up to explain how they would get organised. The train would be leaving tonight from Nairn at eight o'clock, with all the passengers. All the gear would be loaded at Inverness. He invited everyone to get involved, and to join one of the teams. Each team had a leader. They should register with that leader after the meeting. The Intercessor lady was compiling a list of the members who felt called to stay behind. The trains would arrive at eight the next morning in Reykjavik, the capital city. They planned to stay three nights. Images of Iceland were shown as he gave some background on the country. He explained that there was a population of around 260,000. Most of them lived in the area around Reykjavik.

The Intercessor lady addressed the gathering. She told them that Iceland had been a strong opposer to the New Order. They had been a peace-loving country in the past, but many of the Icelanders had taken up arms during the war. Some had made peaceful protests, refusing to fight the forces of the New Order, when they had arrived in heavy numbers in April 2017.

Mark looked at the images of resolute figures: they were digging their defences against a backdrop of dark mountains. He was impressed with their bravery and he was touched, feeling for their sacrifice, as they took on the might of the New Order.

The lady recounted how thousands had died fighting and many, including all their leaders, had been taken away to Level One camps after they had been overwhelmed by the ruthless campaign waged by the New Order. In the following years, many died in their homeland because, as a nation, they were treated in a similar way to Level One Refusers.

Jonathan joined her and told the assembly that the New Order extracted energy from the geothermal sources on Iceland and had developed some of their industry to give them more hard labour. Iceland had been shown to the rest of the world as an example of how fruitless it was to resist the New Order. The Executive ordered that propaganda films of Icelanders suffering hardship should be shown all around the world. When the films were shown, many lost hope of standing against the New Order.

Jonathan invited the lady to lead the community in prayer.

Mark watched her. She was lovely and a little frail, yet there was steel in the way she stood and lifted up her hands. There was passion in her voice as she prayed.

"Father, we commit our plans to you. Lead us by your Spirit in everything we do. Protect us from the Evil One. Your will be done. Your kingdom come to the Icelanders. Accomplish everything you have planned. I declare the Lord's sovereignty over this mission. I release the goodness of God over every soul."

Jonathan thanked her and encouraged everyone to find a team. He read a list with a location for each team meeting.

There was the excited sound of people talking about their next step.

Mark, Sanjay and Johnson went their ways to join a team. Sanjay headed to the Catering team meeting. Johnson joined the Logistics team, in the yard. Mark went over to the Worship and Media team. He found that Jasper was leading the team. They gathered around him.

"I believe worship is going to be central to how we help bring God's love to the Icelanders. Let's pray now and ask God how he wants to use us, then we can go and get prepared."

They prayed in a circle. Jasper asked for God to reveal his plans.

Mark heard different voices sharing, like he had heard in the church back in the city.

"I see the Holy Spirit touching people during the worship," said one.

"I have a picture of people raising their hands."

"The picture I have is that it's like a big party. A celebration."

"I get the words, 'he will come like rain to the dry places.'"

"We need to show images and film as the music plays," said another. "God wants to touch them through their eyes, ears and hearts - all at the same time."

Mark heard several others speak, and then he felt it was his turn to share the picture that was playing in his mind.

There was a pause. Taking a breath, he began to share.

"God is going to heal them through the music," he said. "As we worship his name, people will turn to him. His love is going to flow, as we worship. I get the words: 'many will see, many will hear, and many will trust in the Lord our God.'"

There was another pause.

No one spoke.

Mark opened his eyes to find Jasper looking at him. Jasper's eyes were welling with tears.

"Can I ask you a question?" said Mark politely.

"Of course you can," said Jasper, blinking and sniffing, then raising his eyebrows.

"Have you done this before?" asked Mark slowly, "I mean taking a mission to a whole country?"

Jasper held his gaze for a moment while he pondered.

"Hmm. In the past, the Lord has sent some of us to other countries, or teams of us to different cities, or to some of the other farming communes. This is the first time we are mobilising as an entire camp to go to whole country. This is definitely taking it up a level - a major level!"

There was a murmur of agreement from the others.

Mark glanced around at the faces, and then he asked another question.

"Are you afraid?"

"Afraid?" repeated Jasper. "A long time ago, I agreed with the Lord that my life is his. Whenever he calls, I listen. If he sends me, I do not question. Time and again, he has shown me that he loves it when I am obedient."

Mark nodded, satisfied with his reply.

"Okay people, let's go to it," Jasper said, looking around to the team. "We need all our instruments. And all the media gear we can take. We need to let the Logistics team know what we plan to take. Let's make a list and send it to them. I will contact the churches to ask what they can send us, what we can borrow. We need their support. Let's have our ears open to the Spirit to show us more. We'll have a get-together on the train. Imogen is not with us because she is sorting out medical supplies with Rachel. She will join us on the train. As we work together in love, God will command a blessing, you'll see."

They worked on the list as one group, and then they split up into smaller groups to pack everything, ready for the transport.

Everyone was very intent that morning.

There was a moment when Mark had climbed up a ladder near the meeting area to lift down a speaker. He stopped to survey the team below him as they worked together. He had another flash of *deja vu*. He had had a dream of this very scene: looking down on a group of people who were marked with purpose. He felt reassured that they were in God's will and that he was part of it.

The buzz about camp continued through lunch.

Mark met up with Sanjay and Johnson. Sanjay told them that the Catering team had planned all of the food. They had already prepared the food and drinks for the journey. Johnson told them about the clever storage the Logistics team was using in the yard: boxes fitting into boxes fitting into containers that were to be lifted onto trucks.

The afternoon was spent completing the packing and the loading of the trucks to go to Inverness.

They watched them leave from the yard in late afternoon.

"Don't we need to help unload the trucks at the railway station?" Sanjay enquired.

"No," answered Pete, "the containers will be lifted with cranes straight onto the train. We can go for tea then we can go and get ready."

They joined many others for tea and cakes in the canteen. They were weary and glad to sit down.

They had their devices and they played back some highlights of the day's work for each other to see. They chatted over tea, then went and to shower and pack their things.

Mark felt strange because he realised that this place had quickly become to feel like home. He had not left their room, yet he felt a yearning to return. He opened the window wide so that he could listen for birdsong. He remembered that first morning, waking up in the camp. He thought back to the song on the train: the call to the far away; this time it was for a whole group. They were a large family. This time he was ready to embrace the step into the unknown.

He slipped out and walked down the track and found the place by the stream. It was a peaceful place in the fading light.

In his heart, he said to God, "I am so glad to be alive. Thank you for bringing me here."

A thought came like an arrow into his mind: *The next three days are going to amaze you. Just you wait and see.*

He strolled back to the room.

The others were ready so they made their way with their packs to the yard. There was a line of buses and many people were already taking their places. They helped with loading bags, and then took their seats.

Before long, the convoy of buses swung out onto the road to Nairn. It was dark now. The boy with the curls was in the row in front of them. He chatted to them about what he was bringing and he had lots of questions about what it would be like in Iceland.

"Have you been on the train before?" asked Mark.

"Oh yes, a few times," said the boy. "But only in this country. Never so far."

"Are all the children coming?" asked Johnson.

"Most of us," said the boy, "our teachers are coming too."

The train was waiting for them when they pulled into the station so they loaded and boarded without delay.

"Hi guys, I told you we'd see you again!" said a familiar voice. It was Matt.

He greeted them and showed them their berths.

This time, there was a line of sleeper carriages, one for women, one for men, two more carriages for families.

They had a three-bed berth next to Pete and Stevie. Jasper came along the corridor, checking the list on his device.

"We'll meet in fifteen minutes in the lounge in the end carriage, okay?"

They settled in as the train pulled out of Nairn, heading West and into the night. They found the lounge area with its large windows and comfortable seating. The rest of the worship and media team soon joined them. Imogen and Rachel came and sat beside them.

Jasper addressed the group. He said that he was praying for wisdom on what to prepare.

"I feel that we should have a range of different music. I keep singing some songs that I used to hear in the days long before the war. I feel that the Lord wants to use some songs to remind the older people of the freedom they used to have in the old days."

He played some songs on his device and they discussed how they might be able to use them.

There was one that Mark wanted to hear over again. It was about a child dreaming about paradise. Jasper said that it was written by a British band when he was a boy aged twelve. It had been a huge hit around the world. Jasper said he was praying about some of the words he could change. He shared the song to the devices the others held.

Matt came and joined them.

The media guys said that they felt they should go out and shoot footage of the Icelandic people and landscape to use in the evening meetings.

"We want to communicate to them that God knows them and loves them," explained one of them.

Everyone thought that was a good plan.

"Where will the evening meetings be held?" asked Sanjay.

"We will find out tomorrow," answered Jasper. "It depends a lot on what gear arrives. We are expecting a bunch of stuff from the other churches. There's a second train coming up from the South later tonight."

"How do we get to Iceland?" asked Mark. "It's an island and we are on a train. It's a long way isn't it?"

Matt nodded and smiled.

"That's right. There's a tunnel that connects the North of Scotland all the way over. It was built soon after the end of the war. It's used to connect the power sources on Iceland to the rest of Europe."

He showed them a map on his device.

The tunnels went from the North West of Scotland, due North to the Faroe Islands then North West to Iceland.

"We've been in touch with the other train," added Matt. "They're bringing a lot of gear. There's a team coming with it and all."

They all held hands and prayed. They asked for more wisdom. They asked for all the gifts they would need. They thanked the Lord for everything he would provide. Then they prayed for the Icelanders.

Imogen touched her device so that some words were projected. Jasper started a beat on his device. They synched the devices to play the same song. They sang together a song about a day that would one day come when the Lord would return.

Some of the team bid them goodnight and headed back to their berths.

Jasper played another song from his childhood. It had a faster beat. The words of chorus were about heaven having a plan for each person.

"This song was a huge dance hit in the clubs when I was at school."

Jasper showed them the original lyrics and asked for their help to change them.

"Imagine it is Mark telling his story: how things have changed for him since he left the unit, since God came into his life."

They agreed to keep the words about the Father telling his child not to worry. Mark confirmed that was true for him: God had shown him again and again that he was in His plan; he should not be anxious.

They all worked together until they were satisfied. They had kept as many of the original words as they could, while making it Mark's story.

Mark, Johnson and Sanjay said goodnight and went back to their carriage. They got ready for bed and chatted about the song and about what the next day might bring.

The train had finished loading at Inverness and was now moving again. Out of the window, the lights of the city faded and they were in darkness. The moon was low and the stars were bright.

Mark lay down and they bid each other goodnight, committing each other into God's safekeeping. Mark found the movement of the train lulled him to sleep.

The train moved steadily through the night while they slept. They did not notice the stoppage on the Faroe Islands nor the tilt of the train as it headed into the tunnel suspended in the depths, under the waves of the North Atlantic Ocean.

In his dream, Mark was flying like a bird over the sea.

DAY 12

Morning sounds reached into the berth and the three awoke: people talking; people moving along the narrow corridor of the carriage; the call of seagulls; machinery passing. Someone knocked on their door to rouse them.

They dressed, then raised the blind and looked out of the window.

The train was standing beside some docks. They could see several large fishing boats lying at anchor. The sea was calm. They could see layers of high clouds in the distance to the West. Along the coast, there was a blanket of low cloud.

Sanjay opened the door to the corridor and someone called to him to come for breakfast. They filed out and followed others across the concrete to a large building. The temperature was lower than they remembered at Nairnside.

All three stared up at the building as they approached. It had lines and lines of shaped glass that glinted in the bright morning sunshine. Someone told them it was called The Harp.

Inside, there was a large space with tables and chairs laid out for all of them. They chose what they wanted from the array of food and tucked into a hearty cooked breakfast. All three avoided the pickled fish and some of the other local delicacies.

When everyone was done eating, they were called into the main theatre space for a meeting. Jonathan and Helena were up on the stage with a number of others and welcomed everyone. They introduced the leaders with him, including three Icelanders. Mark spotted the lady who led the Intercessors at Nairnside. They explained that they had a window of three nights for meetings. The team in Central Comms were going to cover them by streaming recent footage of work carrying on as normal over the whole the island. Jonathan said they were excited that the second train had arrived.

"I am particularly grateful that we have Jan and Tomas from Design City Europe with us. I think you are all going to love what they are going to do for us-Jan." Jonathan gestured to a striking man dressed in black. The man rose to his feet and greeted everyone.

"Good morning, brothers and sisters," said the man. "We are delighted to bring you something we can meet in tonight. It is a new design - a prototype tent. We are here to test it, of course. Ordinarily, it would be for a Level 6 gathering. Most of us here are Level 2, but we can keep hush hush about that!"

He winked and smiled. People laughed and some clapped.

"It will be a nice surprise - one of many over these next few days, no doubt. I can tell you it's pretty big so it should fit a good many of us. We are going to raise it at a place called Thingvellir."

Jonathan explained that each team had tasks to do during the day. Each team would be briefed by its leaders. Each team would have some Icelanders attached to it. He outlined what each team would be doing. The plan was to all meet at Thingvellir at five o'clock. He pointed to a huge map of the island.

Helena and the Intercessor lady spoke,

"The Lord has shown us that this is the place where we should hold the meetings. It is very important to the Icelanders. It is where their ancestors used to meet for annual council meetings and festivities a thousand years ago. For the main meeting, we should start at six o'clock. We will start with music and presentations aimed at the children. We should be finished by nine o'clock. Some Icelanders will have a long journey to reach it. Most people live in the city but some live out on farms, spread out all over the country. The people living far away will probably stay with family and friends around the city over the three nights."

"How many are coming?" called out a voice. Mark could not see who spoke.

"We hope a great many," answered Jonathan. "I believe the Lord wants as many as can make it there, to hear our message. Before we go, let us pray together. Susan, please will you lead us."

Mark watched the Intercessor lady from Nairnside step forward. She held out her hands and closed her eyes.

"Lord, we are gathered in your name. We thank you for this opportunity, this door you have opened wide for us. We ask you to guide us all by your Spirit. Help each of us to do our part so that your will is done tonight. We pray for all those coming. Lord, have your hand on them. Prepare their hearts. Speak to them deep in their hearts. Bring them into your kingdom. Let them know who they are in you. We bless you for your care and love. Truly, you are the good shepherd. We trust you, we love you, and we are yours. We pray in Jesus' name.

The room resounded, "Amen."

Mark felt a rush of feelings as she prayed: fresh strength and eagerness to serve; desire to see the Icelanders blessed; thankfulness that he was one of this group; peace that the Lord would lead and guide them.

The meeting was over so they filed out and went to join their teams.

Word came to the Worship team that the trucks were loaded. Mark went out with the team to a coach that was waiting for them, and took his place. The convoy set off through the streets of the city. Mark noticed several buildings that were burnt out ruins. Many walls were scored with bullet holes. They were stark reminders of the fighting during the war. They sat in silence as they passed.

They continued out to the main highway then North West on a main road. Mark stared out at the barren landscape. The morning mist was lifting and he could see black rocks covered in bright green mosses. In the distance there were high ridges and lonely crags and bare summits. There was precious little woodland. They passed fields with ponies but few crops. The villages were small with whitewashed houses. There were a few churches but they were empty and neglected. Some were partly destroyed, demonstrating the rule that the church could not meet in such places.

The convoy slowed as it reached its destination. There were a few old buildings. An old flagpole stood alone further up a slope.

They got off the coach and gathered around Jasper and Imogen. They introduced their local helpers, Petur and Sessilia.

Their guides led them along a path that headed towards a line of cliffs rising up in the middle distance. The group paused by a narrow pool. The water was crystal clear. They had a taste of the water and agreed it was pure and delicious. Petur explained how much of their water was glacial meltwater.

The group continued on a bridge over a river, and up onto a ridge. Looking South, they could see a wide lake stretching a few kilometres. Their guides explained the history of this place.

It was sacred to the Icelanders because this was where their government had begun so many summers ago. Laws were agreed. Disputes were settled. There were feasts. There was music and dancing at these annual gatherings.

They walked over to a wide path and went up to the higher ground. From this vantage point they could see more of the lake. The valley stretched to the right and left. Petur and Sessilia explained that they were standing on the rift between two continental plates. In front of them was the European plate, pulling to the East. Behind and underneath them was the American plate, pulling to the West. They could see that the earth was split with numerous fissures along the boundary.

They looked back at the vehicles of the convoy. A crane was lifting off curious objects and laying them carefully on the ground. There were huddles of figures working around the pieces on the ground. They were all curious to see what they were doing so they headed back. More vehicles were arriving and Mark spotted Johnson with the Logistics team.

As they got closer they saw that the operation was being led by the two men that Jonathan had introduced that morning, Jan and Tomas.

To Mark, the pieces on the ground looked like enormous rolls of plastic - he had no idea what they were for. Under the direction of Jan and Tomas, they were unrolling the lengths of plastic with machinery so that the whole area was being covered. Someone showed them ingenious joining panels that stitched the separate pieces together. There were anchors that were being pinned into the ground. They realised that the anchors prevented the structure from flying away in the wind.

Mark helped with the work so he was absorbed for the next hour.

There was a call for a refreshment break, up by the flagpole. They went up and sat in rows on some stepped seating. Some people had asked Jan and Tomas to explain what was happening, so all heads were turned in their direction.

"Brothers and sisters, we are about to create a structure of geodesic domes, just with the help of some pressured air and water. The structure is based on the hexagon. Each hexagonal cell has tubes that will be filled shortly. The team over there have connected the pumps so, if you watch from here, the process should take about twenty minutes, then we will have space to build the staging and prepare the seating."

As they watched, sections on the ground were lifting and taking shape. To Mark, it reminded him of blowing up balloons as a child.

After about twenty minutes, there was spontaneous applause as the structure completed the process of filling in front of them. It was enormous.

They went over to go inside.

They felt very small. Some of the worship team clapped and shouted to test what the acoustics sounded like. They were standing under a series of domes, the largest being the central one.

A convoy of small forklift vehicles brought in the staging. They set to work fitting it together. Jan and Tomas strolled up and down, giving instructions. Mark looked up later and saw that they were forming a large ring in the centre of the space. Within the centre of ring, there was a circular platform raised higher.

The forklift vehicles brought in seating and flooring.

Later on, they stopped for a picnic lunch when the Catering team arrived. Sanjay joined Johnson and Mark. They told him of the marvel that had been taking form over the morning.

A woman on the stage called out to everyone there,

"Anyone want to hear what this space sounds like?"

There was a cheerful response.

"Hit play," called the woman.

The space filled with an upbeat sound. Some people put down their lunch to do a little dance.

"This place is unbelievable!" said Sanjay. They had not been in such a cavernous space before. Sanjay told them that the catering team was setting up camp to provide food and refreshments. They had lots of fresh food brought over from Scotland plus more provisions from the second train that came up from England.

"We do not know how many might come, but we have got a lot of food!"

The afternoon was taken up with setting up the lights, speakers, electrical equipment and raising the large screens. As the hours passed, more people came to assist, so the work accelerated.

At four o' clock, they were doing the finishing touches. On the central platform, the drum kit and computer controls were set up for Jasper. His kit had clear screens around it. He went up to try it out. He waved at Mark and Johnson.

Stevie came up to them and asked them to follow him. He led them out of the tent and away from the sound of Jasper warming up on the drums.

"One of the teams has set up a camp for the mission team. There are hot showers. It's time to wash and get changed."

They went over to a fenced area with two groups of cabins that had been parked there. Next to the shower cabins there were three large hot tubs.

They showered and then climbed gratefully into the steaming water in one of the tubs. There were surrounded by the rising vapour and a strong smell of sulphur.

"You can't come to Iceland and not have a hot bath!" said Petur, when he joined them. "Sorry, but the rule in Iceland is that you have to shower naked, even at the public baths!"

After a good soak, they went and showered, following Petur's lead, and got dressed into clean clothes and headed back to the meeting tent.

People were gathering from all the teams. The children were there with their teachers. The boy with the curls came over and asked them what they had been doing. They explained how they had watched the tent rise.

"What have you been doing?" asked Johnson.

"We went to two schools and met lots of the kids," the boy replied.

Jonathan and Helena called the meeting to order.

"Well done to all the teams," he began, "this place is amazing! Thank you Jan and Tomas and everyone involved."

There was an enthusiastic round of applause.

They gave them updates on what the teams had been doing during the day. They told them that transport had been arranged to bring people from every part of Iceland. Everyone they had met had spoken about their appreciation for the mission. Word was spreading that people were safe to come to the meetings, and that the cameras had been taken care of. The meetings were going to be recorded and feeds to many churches had been arranged.

Mark thought of the group back in Birmingham, meeting later that night behind those heavy, soundproof doors.

"Now about the meeting tonight," said Helena, "please can we pray together now for how the Lord wants it."

All heads were bowed as she led them in a short prayer. She asked the Lord to put his hand on anyone he wanted to share tonight in the main meeting.

Mark was aware of a burning in his chest.

Jonathan said that he felt that all those who the Lord had chosen would feel heat in their hearts.

"If you feel a burning sensation in your chest, around your heart, please can you put your hand up."

Mark opened his eyes and raised his hand. He was delighted to see that Sanjay and Johnson had their hand up, along with three others.

"Now can we gather round the worship team, the Comms team, the guys doing sound and visuals, and the six who put their hands up and pray for them?" asked Helena.

Mark found himself with about ten people around him, placing their hands on his back and shoulders and chest. There was a mixture of voices as they prayed for wisdom for him, for anointing on his words, for courage and boldness. He felt more heat in his chest, a tingling on his tongue. It felt like God was downloading what he wanted him to share.

After some time praying, Helena led a closing prayer, asking for the Lord to bless every heart, every soul tonight.

She announced that supper was served in the catering area. Mark went with the others and Sanjay peeled off to help serve the food. The team had set up a piazza decorated with tiny lights, trees in tubs, tables and benches. On all four sides, there were serving counters with hot and cold food, and drinks.

Mark and Johnson found a table. They were hungry and gladly ate plates of fish with chips, salads, then cakes with teas and coffee. They were joined by Imogen, Rachel and Susan, the Intercessor lady. They encouraged them with what they would share later.

"I can see that the Lord has his hand on you three," said Susan.

Mark felt the warmth of her eyes on him. "I hear him saying that he is very happy with your willingness to give yourselves wholeheartedly. When you stand up there in front of all those people, he will be right there with you."

Sanjay and some of the catering team came and sat with them. There was excitement in the air, like just before a concert or a big match. Jasper came over to put his arm on their shoulder and tell them that he was eager to see what the Lord would do tonight.

It was time to head over to the meeting so they cleared the table and weaved their way with the rest of the party. The children chased each other in and out of the adults.

As he entered the meeting tent, Mark was astounded to see every row filled with people: families, teenagers and old people; every age was represented. The people were talking in low voices but as the mission team entered, silence fell on the whole space. Mark looked at some of the faces. They seemed to him to have shadows around the eyes and the faces were weather beaten. He felt like they carried years of pain, even the young people.

Jonathan and the leaders went straight up onto the stage. They stood together on a round section of stage that turned slowly so that they could look out at all the crowd.

Jonathan welcomed everyone. He introduced the leaders one by one, and then the team, and explained where they had come from. The Comms team was working at their desks to flash up images and footage on the screens as he spoke.

"The reason we have come is that we believe God wanted us to meet with you."

"Our message is simple," added Helena, stepping forward as she spoke. "God loves you very much. He wants you to know that in a new way tonight."

"He knows what you have been through as individuals and as a country," said Susan.

"We have to come to tell you that the waiting is over," said Imogen.

"The Lord says that this is a new day," said Jasper.

"I encourage you to open your heart to him tonight," said Helena.

"God is spirit. He may touch you in a way that is new to you," said Susan. "You will recognise it is him, because you will feel his love and know truth."

Then one of the Icelandic leaders stepped forward and spoke in Icelandic. Words of the translation flashed up on the screen. He reminded them that at this time a year ago, there was three days of torrential rain. Many rivers were flooded. In the Bible, rain was often a symbol of the Holy Spirit. He said he hoped there would be a flood of the Spirit of God this night.

Jonathan explained that they would like to start with some music and presentations for the children. He invited onto the main stage the children from Nairnside. The leaders moved off and the children arranged themselves. Because the stage was a ring, they were spread out in a big circle.

One boy began, "we want to sing a song to tell you what the Lord is like. Come forward to the front if you would like to."

They sang with no instruments. Mark could see the boy with the curls. As they began to sing, the Icelandic children moved forward to the front. The Comms guys brought up images of their paintings and drawings on the screens as they sang. Mark turned and noticed some of the mothers - both those from Nairnside and some from Iceland - were wiping tears from their cheeks.

At the end of the song, many of the Nairnside children were handed instruments so that the next few songs were accompanied by keyboard, guitars, violins, drums and a flute. The Comms guys flashed up the words so that the Icelandic children could join in the choruses. Some of the songs were more upbeat and so soon the children were jumping up and down, following the actions of the children on the stage.

When they were done, many of the younger children moved to the back of the meeting area where there were sofas and beanbags.

Next there was a film showing the Nairnside children in their Scottish surroundings and their school. The film was narrated by some of the children. They spoke about the Lord, and about what he meant to them.

This closed the children's section of the evening.

Jasper and Imogen walked onto the stage with many of the musicians from Nairnside. Jasper sat on his drum stool and said that they wanted to start with some songs that might remind them of the days before the war.

They started with the song about paradise. It began with keyboards and strings. Imogen sang.

Looking up at her, Mark noticed how she seemed to be totally happy to perform for everyone, like it was what she was supposed to do.

The Comms guys showed footage of some of the Icelandic children they had shot earlier. Mark and the team joined in with the chorus. Several of the Icelandic people nearby sang with them.

Jasper introduced the next song as by a band called Of Monsters and Men. They were an

Icelandic band he remembered from when he was a teenager. Jasper sang with Imogen.

As they played the song, the Comms guys projected footage and images of Iceland and its people, from before the war that they had raided from the Archive. Mark heard some gasps and murmurs from some of the people near him. He could tell that they were moved. The memories stirred up lots of emotions - some of joy, some of pain.

Jasper spoke to the crowd before the third song.

"You might remember a band from the days before the New World Order called Swedish House Mafia. We have changed some words of one of their songs to match the experience of one of our new members."

Mark knew that he was up.

His heart was beating faster, as he climbed the steps onto the stage. From here, the space seemed even more vast now that it was filled with people and their faces were turned towards him. He remembered the words that Susan had said to him over supper. A thought came to his mind: *I am with you.*

He nodded to Jasper.

The keyboard player started with the first chords.

Mark stood in the spotlight and waited.

As he started on the first line, his voice sounded different in such a large space: solitary, vulnerable. The words were projected where he could see them easily. Images came onto the other screens: Mark in his bed in the unit dormitory; the canteen filled with Workers; the streets with Workers walking to their workstations. He kept his gaze on the words in front of him, to save himself from becoming distracted.

The first lines he sang just with the keyboard but then the guy on bass guitar and Jasper on the bass drum came in and he could feel the song was picking up momentum. He tapped his foot. In the corner of this eye, he could see people were responding. Some hands were raised and moving in time with the music. He felt less alone.

The song was gathering pace. He had to raise the volume of his voice. The bass line was stronger. He felt more confident now. The crowd was responding. The people of Jasper's age were leading with arms raised.

The song was building again, as it ran into the first chorus. The louder it got, the more it seemed to fill the space. When the music reached full volume, there seemed to be a change, like a break in a dam. Suddenly, the space came alive, as the guys on lighting flashed colours and shapes in time with the beat. People were jumping up and down in time with the music. It seemed like they were free for the first time in years. Mark's hands went up. Now he was jumping with the crowd.

There was a pause before the second verse. As Mark blinked and looked around; he felt alive. This is it, he thought. This is life. The change that the song talked about was so true for his life. Before, he knew no father. Now, he knew he was a son of the Father.

He sang on, carried along on the flow of the music:

"There was a time,

I was alive, but it was like a dream.

In a hard, hard place,

They looked, but they didn't see your face.

We had to follow,

Every time we heard those three notes…"

This time, when he reached the chorus, he felt with more conviction that he was speaking the words of the Lord to these people. The Lord did not want them to worry. He had a plan for them. He was their true dad. They were children. The grief of the past was behind. It was time to move forward.

Mark pointed to the crowd. He made eye contact with individuals, as if he was telling them that God had a plan for them personally. They seemed to respond even more when he did. He ran and skipped along the stage to engage more of the audience. He made a full circuit, passing the other musicians while Jasper bashed away at the drums on the centre stage.

Mark turned to catch Jasper's eye. They nodded at each other and they went back to repeat the first verse. Mark caught Sanjay and Johnson waving at him and grinned back. This time the whole room seemed to move together to the music. The children had come forward, and many where up close to the stage. It seemed like everyone was agreeing: The Father has a plan for us, for me. They repeated the chorus over and over. It felt like the message was sinking in.

Eventually, the music faded, and the spotlight remained on Mark.

He began to speak.

"Hi everyone, I am Mark."

The crowd waited. The screens showed his words translated.

"Two weeks ago, that was me. I was alive, but I was numb. I had a number, but I had no idea who I was. I did not even know my own name. I did not think for myself. I asked no questions. I followed instructions. Just like all the guys in my unit. That's all we did. We moved when we heard the notes.

"Then one night, I had a dream. I was standing in the desert. I saw a massive sandstorm in front of me. There were steel wheels, like huge saws, carried by the storm. They were spinning with incredible speed. They looked like they could destroy anything in their path. It was awesome. To me, it was a picture of God's power.

"When I woke up, I pushed the dream to the back of my mind. I went back to being a Level Three Worker. I carried on as normal. But then the next night, I had the same dream. This time there was a man standing next to me. He called me Mark. I woke up and thought about the days when I was a child, before I went to school. That morning felt different. I could not shake the feeling that my life was about to change. I wanted to know who I was. It was like I was starting to wake up from a long sleep.

"Then I got a fright. I ran into the guy I had seen in my dream! His name was Sebastian. He asked me if I wanted to know more. I signaled that I did. From that moment, my life has changed in more ways than I can tell you. I moved to the Sick Bay. I came off the gas that they drugged us with in the unit. I joined the church.

"For a while, I thought it was all a dream. But it wasn't. I made friends. I came to know the Lord. I got filled with the Spirit. I had brothers in faith. I discovered my love of music. I love worship. Worship is one of the main ways I love to serve the Lord. I love creativity. I love it that God has made us creative.

"After a few days, we asked the Lord what he wanted us to do. He showed us pictures of us traveling on a train to join a camp. We left the city and went to the mission base in Scotland. These guys welcomed me like I was family. I used to have many fears. I was very worried that we would be caught, but these guys prayed for me, and the Lord has already released me from many fears.

"And now I am standing in front of all of you. I feel alive. I know this is not a dream. This is the real thing. I thank God that he released me. I was a prisoner and I did not even know it. I did not know what freedom tasted like. I cannot thank God enough. I surrender my life to him. If my life ends tonight, I know that I have lived. I know the most important thing: I know who God is, and that I am with him, and he is with me. Nothing else really matters.

"I pray that God does for you what he has done for me. May he heal you and release you, so that you can worship him: worship him in spirit, in truth and with your whole heart. Thank you."

There was a loud cheer and applause as Mark waved to the crowd. He spotted the boy with the curls waving at him. Imogen came up to him and put an arm around his shoulder.

The spotlight left Mark and highlighted Jasper.

Jasper said, "Thank you, Mark! Now, let's sing two hymns together. Your mothers and fathers and your ancestors found encouragement in these hymns."

Mark went to his keyboard. He was happy to see everyone joining in. The first hymn had a Celtic flavor and Mark felt it had an edge of melancholy in this place. It reminded him of the time on the train, the morning they first looked out upon the Scottish moors. The hymn seemed to be affecting the older people profoundly. Some of them became so tearful that they could not stand and sing.

The second hymn was more hopeful, and seemed to lift people's spirits.

Next up was Johnson. The spotlight found him at the front. He walked up onto the stage. Everyone was quiet as he spoke.

"Good evening, everybody, I am Johnson. I want to talk to you about relationship. You were created for relationship, so was I. God is three people: Father, Son and Holy Spirit. They know each other completely. They have unity. We are made in God's image. He created us to know others, and be known by others. Since I came to faith, the same night as my brother Mark, the greatest joy for me is to be among friends and family. Not just that, I pray all the time. I can communicate with my God, my Creator, my Saviour, anytime: morning, noon and night. He is not far away. He is close. He hears all my prayers. He sees me. He sees me here, now. He sees you. He knows you. He wants you to know him.

"Before, in my unit, I was alone. I did not have anyone to truly relate to. I had instructions. I had Supervisors keeping an eye on me. But I had no friendship. No real relationship.

"Then I came across Sebastian. There was something different about him. He seemed to care. One day, he gave me an invitation: "there is someone who cares for you, who wants to meet you. He is God. If you want to meet him, show me..." I wanted that more than anything. The Lord had been giving me hints. Now I had a chance to respond. The journey started for me that day.

"I met Mark and Sanjay in the Sick Bay. We were looked after by a nurse called Michael. As we came off the drugs, we started to talk together. We started to get to know each other. We are now close friends and brothers. We made friends in the church. I loved the fellowship. They told me my name. They knew my name because God had told them.

"We came to the mission camp and found more friends and family. If the Lord asked me to give up my life for these guys, I would not even have to think about it. I love them. I love because he gave me love. He is teaching me how to love. He loves me, so I love others. If he did not fill me up, I would be empty - I would not have any love to give.

"Love is the greatest thing in the world. Love is what makes life worth living. God is a God of love. God is love. Love starts with God. When you experience the love of God, you are changed forever. There is no going back. God wants you to be in fellowship with him, and in fellowship with brothers and sisters. He wants you to be in his family. You are his child. He loves you. He loves all his children. He does not want you to be alone.

"I pray that you experience the love of God tonight. May God bless you. Thank you."

There was loud cheering, applause and some whistles. Mark went over and hugged him before he went down the steps to his place next to Sanjay.

Imogen moved into the spotlight. She thanked Johnson and asked Sanjay to come up. Sanjay joined her on the stage and she withdrew.

"Hello, my name is Sanjay," he began. "My story is similar to Johnson and Mark. I worked in my unit, just like the rest of the guys. I was asleep, just like Mark said. I am someone who wants to know truth. I wanted to know how things really are, so I had a deep dissatisfaction.

I could not put it into words, but that was my need.

"Like the other two, I came across Sebastian in my set tasks. One day, he spoke to me. He told me that all truth comes from God. That shook me.

"The next day, I saw him again. He said that I could meet God. He asked me for a sign. I wanted truth so much, I gave him the sign. I got moved to the Sick Bay and met Michael. Mark and Johnson were there. I went with them to the church. I got saved. I came to God. I received forgiveness. I experienced grace. I was baptised. At last, I could learn truth.

"I am so grateful to God for releasing me. I was a captive. I was in the dark. I did not know truth. Truth is like light. He brought light into my life. There is nothing like the light of truth. The light of God shines in the darkness. This world is very dark. You know that. I know that.

"Jonathan and the team helped us understand the truth about the New Order. How the world is set up. They explained the different levels. They showed us how the world used to be before the war. I had no idea. They wanted us to know the truth. They answered lots of our questions. They even showed us our parents. I had never seen my parents. I did not know where I had come from. There is still so much to discover. We have not been long on this journey, but I am so thankful that I am here.

"The light of God is beautiful. The truth of God sets you free. I love freedom. I feel free. The feeling of freedom that God gives is like nothing else. I have joy because of that freedom. You could put me in prison, but my heart would still be free. No one can take it away.

"I pray that you know truth. I pray that God will reveal truth to you tonight. I pray he sets you free. May he give you joy. Thank you."

Again, there was a swell of cheering and clapping from the crowd.

There were three more testimonies. One was from Joseph, the Level Four man who had come from Hamburg, in Germany. He spoke about getting over the grief of losing family and friends in the war, and his experiences of losing people who had been moved to Level One. The crowd listened soberly and with sympathy.

There were two testimonies from women. One woman was Scottish and spoke of the pain of losing a child, and how God had helped her in her pain. The other woman had been a Level

Three Worker, and she spoke of her experience of being saved and of joining the church. She loved the fellowship they had at the camp. She told them about the night the Lord told them to come to Iceland. She had wept for them. She said she felt God's compassion for them.

The spotlight moved to Jasper. He said that they would like to play some worship songs, and invited the crowd to join in if they wanted to. Mark went over to his keyboard to get ready to play.

They played a series of songs with Imogen and Jasper leading. The common thread was the experience of salvation. The first songs were more about praise - lifting up the name of God. The later songs were more gentle. The last song had the words, "so do not be afraid."

The music faded and came to an end.

Silence fell on the whole crowd.

The lights went dim for about half a minute. Then lights shone onto the main stage. They picked out Jonathan, Helena, an Icelandic leader and Susan, the Intercessor lady.

"We want to pray for you now," said Jonathan.

"We believe that God is going to touch you in a special way," said Helena.

"Many of us have waited a long time for this," added the Icelandic man. "I believe that this is going to be a very special moment for all of us."

Then Susan spoke gently, but with authority,

"I believe that this is what the Lord says to you: 'I know all the hardship you have endured. I know the pain you have had. You have suffered enough. Now I come to you. It is time for you to know salvation. It is time for you to feel joy at last.'"

They held out their hands towards the crowd. There was quiet for a short time. Mark closed his eyes and waited. Then he heard people starting to cry.

Jonathan asked the whole team to come onto the stage and hold out their hands. They all went up, including many of the children. They formed a circle, looking out in every direction. They stretched out their hands and prayed.

The sound grew. Some of the crowd were crying, others were calling out, still others were moaning as if they were wounded or in pain.

Then Jonathan spoke,

"Anyone who calls on the name of the Lord will be saved. Salvation is when you cross over.

Jesus said, 'repent because the kingdom of God is near.' The kingdom of God has come to you tonight. The Spirit is here. It is time to repent. To repent is to turn. It's a change of mind and a change of direction. All you have to do is say yes in your heart. Then say sorry if you have been living for yourself, if you have been ignoring God, if you have resisted him. He says that he stands at the door. He knocks on the door of our hearts. We have to let him in - he will not force his way into our heart. He only comes in if you open the door. Do not be afraid. He is good. He is kind. He is gentle. He is strong.

"I encourage you to say yes to God, tonight. Come into his kingdom. Come under his wing. Come and know the truth. Come and know that you are loved. Love is stronger than anything - even death. Come and submit to him as Lord. His name is above every name. He is the Lord of lords. He is the King of kings. There is no one worthy, like he is worthy. He died for you. He paid the price to bring you into God's presence. He offered the sacrifice. Humankind was separated from God through what Adam did. Humankind was reconciled, reunited with God, through what Jesus did. Jesus was blameless.

He took the blame for us. When he died, he said, 'it is finished' - it's paid for. It was the most important day in history.

"He redeems you. Someone sold into slavery could be freed, if a relative paid the redemption price. He did that for you, once for all. He paid the price. It cost him his life. Every single one of you who calls on the name of the Lord tonight, will be saved. Believe in him, and cross over from death to life.

"I pray that God will come to you tonight. Lord, reveal your salvation to your children. Come Spirit of God. Many will see. Many will fear. Many will put their trust in you."

As soon as he said these last words, there was an invisible wave that swept through the whole space. It started at the front, near the stage, and went out like ripples on a pond, all the way to the back. People were dropping to their knees and falling down on the ground. Many people were calling out, "Jesus." Some lay on the ground like they had been knocked out. The volume coming from the crowd increased. Mark thought it was like a God-ordained chaos: the din was like nothing you would get in the Level Three city. Compared to the order in his unit, this was happy mayhem.

The meeting was officially over, but for several hours there were people praying together in small groups. Mark, Johnson and Sanjay spent much of that time moving through the crowd, laying hands on people and praying with them.

When it was close to midnight, they were sitting on one of a line of coaches, heading back to the city. They were grateful to wash and to fall into their beds on the train.

That night, Mark dreamt of the meeting: he was dancing on the stage with the others in front of an exuberant crowd.

DAY 13

They woke in the morning when the carriage came to life. They washed and dressed, then followed others to breakfast, as they had done the day before.

At the meeting, Jonathan, Helena and the other leaders shared the news of the impact of the meeting the night before. They told them that many churches had sent encouraging messages and they played several for them to see. Mark and the others were delighted to see the excitement in the message from the New Birmingham church sent by John, Sebastian, Michael and the others. They had watched the entire evening meeting. They could not contain their joy.

"Mark, Johnson and Sanjay - you were awesome!" called Sebastian to the camera.

There was news that another train had arrived that morning with more supplies.

The leaders outlined what each of the teams were planning to do that day. The whole team was going to meet at five o' clock, as they had the day before. The Worship group was going on a tour with Petur and Sessilia.

After some prayers of thanks, the meeting ended and Jasper's team followed their guides out to the coach.

"We have some treats in store for you today," Petur told them.

Their coach drove out on a highway heading South East.

Someone had asked Petur to tell them about what life was like before the war, when he was at school so he told them stories of his childhood in Hafnarfjordur. His parents both worked. His father was an engineer, making prosthetic limbs, and his mother worked in a hotel. In the winter, they would skate on a nearby lake. In summer, they could play football outside. He loved to go to the public baths and go on the waterslides.

Their first coffee stop was in an old shopping centre in a town near the coast. There was a slab of glass over a large crack in the floor, where an earthquake had split the building many years ago. They could stand with one foot either side of the crack.

The local people they came across all wanted to shake their hands, and thank them for the meeting the night before. Some people asked for them to lay hands on them and pray for them.

"The best night we have had for a long time," said one older man.

They drove on past fields and onto a wide plain covered in black stones. A high hill rose up on its own. They drove down a track to its base. The coach parked and they all spilled out to climb up to its summit. There, they stood and looked out to the views in every direction. To the South, the sea glistened. To the North, the land rose up to a mountain covered in a glacier. There was no sign of movement except the wind blowing on the tufts of grass. It looked like a desolate wilderness.

"This hill we are standing on is an extinct volcano," said Sessilia.

"This landscape reminds me of a story I read when I was a lad," said Jasper. "There was a black land called Mordor."

They descended down the steep path and climbed back on the coach. They drove on to a place with some high, black cliffs that rose high above the flat plain that stretched towards the sea. The coach pulled over and Petur led them towards a high waterfall. A path went around under the cliffs, into a shallow cave at the rear of the waterfall. Mark gazed up at the overhang and water raining down.

"Who is coming in?" called Jasper as he ran forward.

"Not me!" replied Imogen.

Mark pulled his clothes off with some of the others and they waded out into the pool. The water was up to his shoulders at the base of the waterfall. The water beat down on them from the high cliff top. It was very cold, but it was exhilarating.

"The water comes from a glacier!" shouted Sessilia, over the loud sound of the water landing on the pool. "Are you guys completely crazy?"

They were shivering now, so they retreated to where Imogen and Sessilia were holding some towels. They had a run along the bottom of the cliffs to warm up. Petur had flasks of hot tea for them back at the coach.

A few kilometres further down the highway, they turned off towards another line of high cliffs. They separated the coastal plain and the high plateau inland. There was another beautiful waterfall. In the bright sunshine, the spray created a vivid rainbow. They stood in a line and stared at it for a while. Mark was mesmerized by the quantities of water gushing off the top of the cliff.

Then they took lots of photos and film. Petur suggested that they try drinking the water, but not to wade in again. Mark picked up some of the smooth black stones and stuck them in his pocket. The water tasted incredibly pure and refreshing. There was a small hamlet of old buildings. They had their picnic lunch out of the wind, in the old schoolhouse.

The coach driver took them down to the coast. They went to the beach and threw countless smooth stones into the breaking waves. Mark, Johnson and Sanjay had never been to a beach before. They pulled off their boots and socks, and ran in and out, trying to avoid the reach of the freezing, foaming water.

They climbed up and stood on the cliffs, with the strong breeze in their hair, and looked out to sea. Waves pounded the shore, far below. Mark loved the sight of the majestic North Atlantic Ocean: thousands of miles of open sea;

line upon line of waves riding with the wind towards them; a clear sky stretched high over them.

Looking along the coastline, they could see jagged rocks sticking up in the sea, under a constant onslaught from the waves. They stood out darkly against the pale water.

"We call those rocks 'dragon's teeth,'" said Sessilia.

"What an incredible country!" said Johnson.

The others nodded.

They had a race back to the coach.

It was time to head back to Thingvellir. The coach drove through more bleak and empty landscape until they crested a ridge, and they could see the long lake and the meeting tent in the distance. There were more trucks parked and the whole site was a hive of activity. They were curious to hear what was happening.

They walked towards the catering piazza. They passed new tents and cabins, then a group who were engrossed in setting up something. Jasper spotted Stevie and called to him.

"Hi Stevie," he said, "what is going on here, matey?"

Stevie came over and greeted them.

"Take a wee guess," he answered with a cheeky grin.

"It's for more catering?" tried Johnson.

Stevie shook his head.

"It's for prayer teams?" asked Mark.

"Na'," said Stevie. "Tomorrow morning, this whole area is gonnay be one massive theme park! All the kids who come are going to have the time of their lives. Look over there."

He pointed to a colourful structure at the top of the hill, above the cliff, beyond the meeting tent.

"There are slides running all the way from the hilltop up there, all the way to the lake. Over there you will find machines that spin you around. You would nay believe the kit they brought from the train this morning!"

Stevie called to the others in his team to break for tea, and they made their way through more installations to the catering piazza. Mark was glad to find quantities of hot tea and a range of cakes and tasty treats. They sat together and talked about their trip. Sanjay, wearing his apron, came and sat with them.

Something about the view of the lake drew Mark's gaze. The sunshine glittered brightly on the water. He went quiet, as he listened to the excited chatter around him, silently staring out across the lake, towards the South West.

Something moving in the distance drew his attention.

"What is that?" he asked suddenly.

He pointed.

The others stopped talking and looked in the direction he was pointing. There were small dark shapes moving towards them across the lake. At first, Mark thought they were birds. They came at speed. They were moving too fast to be birds. The dark shapes came hurtling towards them in formation, dipping low near the water, then soaring up over their heads and turning. They made a few circles around them, then slowed and came down to land on the grass, close to where they were sitting. There were five people in black suits with what looked like wings sprouting from their shoulders.

Everyone in the piazza had stopped to watch.

The one nearest them, pulled off a helmet, and called over cheerfully,

"Are we in time for tea?"

Imogen gasped, and put her hand up against her heart.

"Archie?" her voice was uncertain.

"Hi, darling sister," came the reply.

The figure was walking towards them.

"Sorry we did not let you know we were com…"

He did not finish his sentence, because Imogen had sprinted over to him and had jumped into his arms, flinging her arms around his neck.

"Archie, Archie, Archie" she kept repeating. She was laughing.

Jasper had joined them now, and he had thrown his arms around the man.

Mark and the others walked over to greet the visitors.

Jasper turned to introduce them.

"Guys, this is Archie. Our little brother."

Mark looked into the handsome face below the blonde locks: the brown eyes, and the warm smile. The handshake was firm and friendly.

"You guys are total legends!" Archie said. "Man, we could not do anything but watch the whole thing, last night. What a night! O my Lord! We woke up early this morning and we pleaded with the Lord to let us come over here. It has taken us most of the day to get here!"

"Where have you come from?" asked Johnson.

"We have been at a mission base in the mountains of Northern California."

He introduced the other four.

Imogen was embracing a woman called Caley.

"How are my parents?" the woman asked.

"They will be here soon," Imogen replied.

"Come on. What are these things?" Jasper was prodding Archie's suit.

"Jet suits, bro'," he said. "They are stealth, very fast. Handle brilliantly. They're on loan. Naturally. I must give you a try later."

They climbed out of the suits and came and sat at the table, where they all chatted animatedly.

Sanjay and two others on his team plied them all with food and drinks.

Jasper spotted Jonathan and Helena approaching with the leaders.

"Heads down, you guys!" he whispered quickly.

Imogen got up and went over to Helena.

She took her arm.

"There's a surprise," Mark heard Imogen saying.

Helena looked towards them. Her eyes met those of the woman.

"Caley?" she called, uncertain.

Caley leapt to her feet and ran to them. Arms and heads knitted together. Mark loved watching the way they embraced. Helena was laughing and crying at the same time. Jonathan joined in. Then one of the male visitors stood up and went to them.

"Nathan!" Jonathan and Helena said together.

Mark watched them share hugs, tears and more laughter. He could not help but smile.

Jasper explained that Caley and Nathan were Jonathan and Helena's children. They had been at the Nairnside camp for many years until they had been called to go to North America, about two years before. Archie had gone to join them a year ago.

Jonathan and Helena came and sat with them. They traded questions. The visitors wanted to know how it had felt at the meeting, the night before.

"Come on, Mark. What was it like up there when you sang 'Don't you worry'? asked Archie with a friendly grin.

"At first, I felt very alone," replied Mark, "standing up there in the spotlight, everyone looking at me. But then I remembered the words Susan had spoken to me at supper. By the end, I did not want to stop. It was amazing, seeing the reaction from the crowd."

"He is well into music and we are happy to have him in the worship team," added Jasper, winking at Mark.

"Not bad choice of song, for you!" Archie kicked Jasper's chair.

"Archie, have you brought your toothbrush?" Jasper asked mischievously.

"Are you kidding?" retorted Archie, "I was hoping that you brought a spare!"

"Funnily enough, I did! I suppose you are going to nick my clothes too. You can share my berth on the train. What is mine is yours. It'll be like old times," said Jasper.

"Just love you," said Archie, smiling, "have you got something for me to play tonight? Don't expect me to sit on my derriere at the back!"

"We will fix you up, if you can remember what to do," said Jasper.

Archie playfully made like he was going to throw a punch his way.

"Now, you two, remember bed by ten," said Imogen, poking fun at them.

Sanjay came over and told them that supper was served.

They filled their plates with food from the buffet. The banter continued throughout the meal. Everyone was excited, anticipating the meeting.

After supper, they gathered in the tent with all the team and helpers.

Jonathan and Helena welcomed everyone, and then they called up Nathan and Caley, to introduce them.

Different leaders shared the news of the day. They showed some recorded messages from churches across Europe. John, in New Birmingham, summed up how they felt when he said,

"It is hard to put in words how delighted we are to see the Lord at work in you, and to see Him going after a whole nation like this."

Jan explained that the area would be open as a theme park for children the next day. The teams had worked hard to set up the rides. The plan was to open at eleven o'clock the next morning. They would need volunteers to look after the rides and to help in the many activities. They planned to organise all the helpers at the morning meeting, the next day.

Susan stepped forward and called them all to pray.

There was a mix of voices, as some prayed in English, some in Icelandic, and some in other tongues.

Then Susan addressed the gathering and said, "Today, as Intercessors, we bathed the meeting tonight in prayer. We contacted other Intercessor groups around the world. Our belief is that tonight's meeting is about God revealing his power to heal. Can we say 'Amen' to that together?"

The reply came with passion from all the men, women and children,

"Amen!"

They repeated the word two more times.

Mark felt a solid confidence in his gut that God was going to do marvelous things that night.

They all went to the entrances to welcome people as they arrived. Mark enjoyed seeing the range of faces and ages. Many people wanted to shake hands or even give him a hug.

He did not notice the time pass until the meeting tent was full. He went with Johnson to their place among the team, beside the stage.

Jonathan and Helena started the meeting with a welcome.

"Last night was one of the best nights of my life," he announced.

"I was so happy to see the Lord touching so many of you," Helena added.

The meeting got underway with some songs for the children. The Nairnside children led the worship. Mark felt like he could taste the growing excitement in the atmosphere.

After a number of songs, Helena invited some people to come up and share what they had experienced the night before. There was a line of people at the stage; they took it in turns to tell what they had felt.

Mark liked hearing about one boy who said that when they prayed he had seen a man surrounded by light, reaching towards him. An old man said that he had cried his eyes out for the first time for years. He thought that God had turned his back on him and his family - all Icelanders. The love of God he felt had melted his heart. A young woman said that she had always felt so much fear for people in power, and so she had cowered away from any mention of a powerful God. God had appeared to her in a way that was so gentle. As she spoke, she kept stopping to wipe away tears. Her story affected many others in the crowd. Mark felt deep sympathy for them. These people had been profoundly bruised by the New Order. Helena held the woman in her arms.

"A beautiful thing about the Lord is that he knows all about our hurt," encouraged Helena. "He feels for us. His empathy is like none other. If you are like bruised reed, he will not break you."

It was time for worship and so the team, with Archie, took their places. Someone had set up a guitar for Archie.

Jasper and Imogen began with some gentle songs. One was about God opening eyes and giving faith. Another was about Jesus being a healer. Archie came and stood with Mark.

The next song went, "We all need compassion,

and love that never fails,

let love fall on us.

Everybody needs forgiveness,

the mercy of a Saviour,

A hope for all the earth."

These words seemed to have an uplifting effect on the way people were feeling, so they went onto some more upbeat songs. The crowd clapped along with the beat from Jasper's drums. Mark followed on his keyboard. It was a thrill for him to be involved on the stage, where he could see the response of the crowd easily, and see the other musicians play. He loved the way Jasper and Imogen seemed so sensitive to the mood of the meeting. The last song invited the Lord to release his power so that everyone might see his glory.

At the end of the song, the lights went down and spotlights fell on Helena, Jonathan and Susan.

"Now we are going to ask God to give some words for you, and then we will call people to come forward for prayer," said Jonathan. "We believe that God wants to demonstrate his power to heal tonight. When one of our team feel God speaking to them about one of you, they will come up and share it. We would like that person to come forward to receive what God wants to give you. Get ready. You are going to see some amazing things."

Susan then prayed, asking God to release words to the team.

Mark was standing with Johnson and Sanjay in the team area. He closed his eyes and stretched out his hands. In his heart, he prayed for wisdom for the team.

Rachel was the first up. She spoke slowly so that people could understand her accent.

"I see a woman," she said. "You have suffered loads of pain from when you was a girl. For many years you hated yourself. You thought about suicide many times. You've got loads of tattoos, all over your body. Each tattoo expresses your hopelessness and your despair. God wants to show you that there is hope. There is healing. He loves you. He says to you, come. Come now and receive my love. You came here tonight thinking like, 'God would never notice me in a crowd this big.' He knows you but. Your name is Olina. Where are you, sweetheart?"

A woman with long dark hair was threading her way down from near the back of the crowd. Her hair fell over her face. She made her way onto the stage next to Rachel. Helena and Imogen came and stood with them.

"Are you Olina, pet?" asked Rachel.

The woman nodded. Mark could now see her face was already streaked with tears.

"Well, darlin', I have good news for you," continued Rachel. "Can I pray for you? Because God has something special for you, pet."

Then, stretching out her arm, she made a declaration, with passion in her voice, "In the name of Jesus, I declare healing in your heart. Today is restoration day for you, Olina. Come Holy Spirit. Cleanse and heal this daughter of the King!"

The woman began to shake, starting with her legs, and then it got more powerful until she was bouncing on the spot. Then, with a cry, she fell backwards. Jonathan and two other men caught her and laid her on the floor. Rachel and Imogen knelt next to her and continued to pray for her.

"Sometimes the power of God makes us shake," said Helena. "People used to call it, 'slain in the spirit' in the old days."

Pete was the next from the team to go up.

"There is a man here who was injured in the fighting in the war. Your name is Hakon. Your right leg is as stiff as a post."

There was a man already making his way forward. He walked awkwardly, with a stick.

"God wants to sort your leg for you tonight," added Pete. He embraced the man as he reached the stage. He asked him a few questions - his name and how his leg had been injured. The man said that he had been shot in the fighting.

He had eventually been carried away from the fighting to be treated in hospital, but by then the leg had already got infected.

"Can I pray for you?" asked Pete.

The man nodded. A chair was brought for the man to sit.

"Thank you Lord for the miracle you are going to do now," said Pete. He knelt and placed his hand on the man's leg. "Be healed in Jesus' name."

There was no shaking. The man said he could feel heat where Pete was touching him. Pete asked him to try walking. The man started to walk. His stride was natural and easy. He stopped and jumped up with his arms up.

The crowd burst out with cheering and clapping.

One of the Nairnside children went up to Helena then addressed the crowd.

"There is an old lady," he said, "your name is Frida. You have problems breathing. Your breaths are really short."

An old woman with silver hair came slowly forward. She was helped up onto the stage.

The boy laid hands on the lady.

"Your lungs are healed in Jesus' name. Breathe in the breath of God," said the boy.

"I can breathe!" called out the lady.

There was cheering and clapping from the crowd. Some people called out her name.

Then Mark saw Becky move up to stand beside Helena.

"Someone called Lara is here," she said. "You have tried to have children many times. Come down now and received healing from God."

A lady came up shyly.

Becky placed one hand on her back and one on her front. She prayed for healing. The lady went over like a felled tree. She was caught, and Becky and some women prayed for her while she lay on the stage.

The woman with Rachel was now standing with her by a tub of water.

Rachel spoke so that all could hear, "God wants to wipe away your tattoos. If you come and be baptized, you will be washed clean in Jesus' name."

They went down into the water. Rachel helped the woman as she went under. She came up with her arms raised. The woman pulled her sleeves up to show her arms.

"The tattoos are gone!" Rachel exclaimed.

The crowd clapped as the two women hugged.

One of the guys in the band went up. He had a shaggy red beard. Mark knew his name - Joz. He was emotional as he spoke; his voice was unsteady.

"There is musician here who used to play keyboard in a band a long time ago. The band was famous around the world. Your name is Kjartan. In the war, they did a terrible thing to you. You were punished for being part of the resistance. They cut off your hand so that you could not play music. They showed you in their films. They were cruel and humiliated you and your people. Can you come up please?"

Joz had to wipe his tears. The crowd went very quiet. A lone figure was making his way up to the front. As he came closer, Mark could see that he held one arm as if he was trying to hide it.

Joz hugged him and asked him if he could pray for him.

"I believe God says this to you: 'I am so sorry this happened to you. I know what it did to you. Now I want to give you back your hand.'"

Then Joz said, "There is nothing impossible for God. Let this arm be whole in Jesus' name!"

The man held out his arm. There was his hand!

He held out the other hand, as if he might be dreaming.

The crowd gasped, then laughed with him, and then applauded.

Mark felt like a sense of awe had come upon the meeting.

The man was speechless. After a few moments, he spoke,

"This is incredible! I can hardly believe it. I want to thank the Lord. He is a God who heals! þakka þér fyrir að lækna mig. Thank you for healing me."

The crowd erupted with cheering.

Kjartan raised his hands. "And now," he continued, "can I play something on a keyboard? I want to see if this hand works! If the others are here, can we play something for you maybe?"

Jasper and Imogen beckoned the other band members, as they were making their way down. Jasper took the drummer over to the central stage with his drums, and handed him his sticks, while Joz took Kjartan to a keyboard.

The crowd fell silent and waited.

"This song," said Kjartan, "was one of our best."

He started playing some simple notes, like a child might play.

The crowd seemed to sigh, as one. A lady with a violin started to play, and then the bass and drums came in. The singer of the band started singing. His voice was pitched high. Mark did not understand the words; he followed the translation on the screens. The music slowed as if it was stopping then it picked up into a crescendo with more strings. The Comms guys showed some images and footage of the band's concerts when they were younger and some clips from the original music video. Mark could see that some of the older Icelandic people could not stop from weeping. The song gathered momentum with more string and wind instruments joining in.

The music faded and ended with Kjartan playing the same notes that started the song. He played them over and over, as if he wanted to give his hands the chance to remember what it felt like to play.

He stopped and the whole room stood to applaud the band.

Kjartan stood up and bowed, and waved with both hands held high.

Helena clapped with everyone, and then as calm returned, she spoke.

"Fantastic, thank you so much. God said he was going to flood this place with his healing power. Now, we want to pray for everyone. Our team is going to move among you now. If one of our team has a word, they will speak it out from the stage. If you hear something that is for you, come and meet our team here. We will direct from here."

Then Susan prayed,

"God - Father, Spirit, Jesus - we bless you for what you are doing. Come and do more. Let every heart be touched. Let the healing flow. Come Balm of Gilead."

Mark teamed up with Johnson. They approached groups and families, asked them what they needed healing for, and prayed. They saw a boy with bone problems in his legs healed; a mother with a skin condition was healed in front of them; several people with old injuries were sorted; a boy who was deaf could hear, after they prayed; an old man with a bent back was straightened.

He was delighted to see the joy on the faces of the people, when they received healing. In his heart, he kept blessing the Lord for letting him be part of this.

Eventually, Jonathan announced that it was getting very late. He called the team onto the stage for one last, blasting prayer. They all stood around the stage, in a ring, facing out to the crowd. They all held out their hands towards the crowd.

Jonathan asked the Spirit to come. He called for healing on the nation.

As they prayed, many were shaking and crying out.

The meeting was over.

There was plenty of excited chatter on the coach on the way back into the city. People shared their experiences of praying amongst the crowd. Sanjay had teamed up with a man in the Catering team. There had been a child in a wheelchair that had climbed out and walked without help, after they prayed.

At the train, they had a wash and fell into bed. Soon they were asleep.

That night, in a dream, Mark saw himself sitting at a table, staring out of a window. He saw a tall and powerful angel nudge him, and tell him that God wanted him to write a song. At first, Mark asked if he knew enough about music. The Lord said that he would show him everything he needed to know.

DAY 14

That morning at breakfast in The Harp, Mark went over to where Jasper was sitting. He asked to sit with them. Imogen looked at him keenly from across the table. Archie sat beside her. They asked him how the meeting had gone for him, the night before. He told them about how Johnson and he had prayed for different people, and the results they had seen.

"It's amazing," said Jasper, "to think you have been in this only about two weeks! Now, I am guessing you have a question. Fire away, matie."

Mark smiled and said, "Well I do have a question. I feel a kind of nudge from the Spirit. He says he wants me to write a song."

"I'm not surprised," replied Jasper, putting a hand on his shoulder, "you are a worshipper. It's in your spiritual DNA. It was a matter of time. Plus you have my sister praying for you day and night. She can't seem to stop!"

Imogen made a face at him from across the table.

Mark told them about the dream he had had during the night.

"Okay, I get it. Let's pray now," said Jasper, and without hesitating, he said, "Lord, thank you for all the gifts you give us. Thank you for what you are doing in Mark. We ask you give him wisdom. Help him to hear you clearly. We say yes to the song you want to give. Bring it on, Lord."

After breakfast, they went into the meeting. There was news of more healings. There were messages from the churches across Europe.

The leaders spoke of the need for helpers at the park today.

They headed out to board the coaches and the convoy headed out to Thingvellir.

Jan and Tomas were already there with some of the team. They split them all up into groups and took them on a tour of the park. There were lots of small stands where you threw things at targets, or fired water guns. They went to check out the rides, and everyone who wanted a go on each, did so. There were merry-go rounds, rides that lifted and spun you, and many more.

There were slides that started high at the top of the site - faster slides were coloured black, medium were coloured red, easier slides were blue, green and yellow. Jan led Mark's group up there to ride the slides.

Mark tried a red slide - it was his first time. He hurtled down past the meeting tent, over a hump, and spilled out right down by the lake.

There was a set of curious contraptions at the lakeside.

The group gathered there.

"What is this?" they asked Jan.

There were six arms in a line, each with a sling.

"Watch this!"

He asked for a volunteer.

Sanjay was the first to step forward.

Jan asked him to sit on a rubber seat with a back that went up above his head.

"Are you ready?" he asked with a wink at the others.

"I think so," said Sanjay.

Jan pressed a button.

The arm suddenly flicked forward in a blur of movement.

Sanjay was catapulted high into the air across the lake, like a small ragdoll. The others gasped, thinking he would be hurt if he hit the water at such speed. They peered into the distance. The tiny figure of Sanjay had hit squarely on one of six enormous screens rising up from lake. The material was so light that one could easily miss it. The small black figure was sliding down to a platform in the water. The screen was angled so that it slowed his fall. He landed on inflated cushions and waved back at them. They could hear his excitement across the water.

"Wow!" breathed Mark.

"How is he going to get back?" asked Johnson.

"Easy," said Jan.

Someone was helping Sanjay onto a thing like a jet ski.

He came racing back across the water towards them up to a landing stage nearby. The jet ski slowed and stopped automatically.

Archie was looking closely at the jet ski.

"I see there's no smoke from the jet ski. How is it powered?" he asked.

"Bio-fuel and solar. There is a submerged electro-magnetic line to guide it," replied Jan pointing to a line of little lights under the water.

Sanjay was brimming with excitement as he ran up.

"You have to try this!" he said.

They sat in the seats: Mark, Johnson, Sanjay, Archie, Jasper and Joz.

Jan counted them down and pressed a button.

The arms flicked forward and they went sailing through the air, crying out to each other.

Mark saw a blur of water below him, and then his speed was slowed as he landed in the screen and he slid down in a heap onto the cushions.

They were all still laughing as they were shown how to use the jet skis to come racing back over the water.

"Like it?" asked Jan.

"Love it," they answered.

It was getting close to opening time, so they were shown where to go by Jan.

Mark started off on a stand.

Young children soon came bouncing up with their parents in tow, to shoot the water guns. They had to fill up containers shaped like brightly coloured balloons. When the water filled the container, a hatch opened and six little boats raced around a course to a finish line, in front of them. The winner out of the six contestants received a prize.

Later on he was relieved by another team member. He walked to the piazza to get some lunch. He sat and ate food with several others. He spotted Jasper and asked him if he could go and try out the song that he had been humming all morning. Jasper smiled and told him to remember to give the words to the Comms guys. Mark spoke to one of the coordinators to check he was not needed, and left.

Mark slipped into the main tent and waved at the Comms guys on his way up to his keyboard. He recorded the song by singing into the microphone and pressed some buttons to find out what notes he was using. The computer guided him on chord options. He tried a few different options. He pressed 'Complete' when he was happy. It had produced the lyrics in text by recognising his voice.

He called over to the Comms guys to ask them to give him some amplified sound. They gave him the thumbs up.

He played the chords as he was guided by the lit colours on the keys, and sang his lyrics. Unbeknown to him, Jasper had arrived and was now talking with the Comms guys. Mark sang the song to the end before he noticed Jasper coming up to him.

"Hey Mark, that sounds cool," he said. "Let me try and follow you on the drums."

He showed Mark how to share the song for the rest of the band, and for the Comms guys. He went over to the drums and then asked Mark to play it again.

This time Jasper came in with drums when he reached the chorus. It sounded great to Mark. They played to the end then Jasper beckoned him over to the Comms hub. They played back the song a few times. They discussed ways they could bring in other instruments. Jasper played with the computer for a while until he was satisfied.

"You've got a nice wee song there, buddy," he said approvingly.

He wanted to show Mark some other songs that they could play later so they went back to Mark's keyboard to help him get familiar with the songs. He played him different versions of some songs and they practiced them.

"Look, it's time for tea!" said Jasper at last.

"Already!" said Mark, surprised. "Thank you so much for your help."

"Time flies when you do something you love," answered Jasper, giving him a knowing look. He waved to the Comms guys and they strolled back to the piazza.

Imogen wanted to know what they had been doing so they explained.

"That's brilliant," she enthused. She gave them both a hug.

The park had been a big success with young and old so they all ate supper later than the previous nights. The light in the sky was already fading but the piazza was lit with hundreds of tiny lights.

Jonathan stood up and thanked everyone for their help. They would go straight into the main meeting tonight.

"We believe we are going to see God blast them with his power tonight," he declared to a positive response from the whole team.

As they headed to the main tent, Mark could see that families had brought picnics so they could stay the whole day. Groups were dotted about over the whole site.

From every direction, there were now steady streams of people moving to the entrances of the main tent.

Soon the place was full and the meeting could begin.

The leaders stood together on the section of stage that turned slowly.

Jonathan spoke to the entire gathering.

"Did you have a good time today?"

There was a loud response from the crowd.

"Friends, I want to say a few things before we get the party started tonight. We came here from Scotland because we heard God's call, and we were ready to obey. God loves it when we are willing and obedient. We could have said, 'Look, we are only three hundred - what can we do?' But we had the support of our friends in the churches. We were joined by Franz and Joseph. Then Jan and Tomas said they would come.

"We are just servants. Some of us sing; some of us play music; some of us cook; some of us put stuff together. We are servants - that's all we are. But we serve the living God, the Creator of all things."

There was a cheer from the crowd that extended into a roar. Jonathan stood with the other leaders, with arms raised in response.

Then Helena said, "I feel like there are a few people here who are dying to share something. Your heart is fit to burst. Give me a wave."

Four arms went up immediately and waved at her. The leaders pointed to them. Helena invited them to come down and share.

The first lady came up and excitedly shared how she had had chronic back pain for fifteen years, and it had lifted off in the final prayer blast, the night before. She had ended up on the floor. She said it felt like a troop of dwarves were jumping on her back. When she was able to stand, the pain had gone.

The second lady was the woman with the tattoos, Olina. She looked completely different to Mark. Her dark hair was pulled back so he could see her face. She shared how God had healed her when Rachel and the others had prayed.

"It felt like God was filling me with bright light. All the darkness had to leave. I feel like a new person. I am happy for the first time in my life. When I got home I checked in the mirror. All the tattoos are gone! It's like they have been washed off!"

She laughed and did a little dance, and then hugged Helena.

Rachel went over to hug her at the bottom of the stairs.

Helena beckoned them both back up.

"Rach, what did you pray and how does it feel now?"

"Well, see," began Rachel, "I just let the Lord lead me. He gave me bits of Scripture to speak over her. I declared that she was a daughter of the King, and a princess. She is loved with an everlasting love."

"And how does it feel, seeing her now?" asked Helena.

"I just… I'm just so happy." Rachel's voice ended with a quiver, and she started to cry. The two women retreated down the steps, arms around each other's shoulders.

"Bless you, darling," said Helena. "We are so blessed to be here. To minister to you all. To serve the Lord like this. Now, who else came down?"

The third testimony was from a young man. He shared how he had had so much hatred in his heart for the New Order, it had taken over his life.

"I left my family and my home and I joined a gang. We lived in a blown out building. We used to roam around the empty parts of the city, smashing things and vandalising, getting drunk and living in squalid conditions. Hatred consumed all of us.

"Then last night, I found one of your team, Jim. He prayed for healing in my heart. It was like being given electrical shocks. I shook for ages. At the same time, my heart was being changed. I went back home to my family last night. I am with them tonight."

He turned and waved to his family further back, under one of the domes.

The crowd gave him a rousing cheer.

The fourth man to come up to Helena was Kjartan.

"Hi Kjartan," said Helena, "that was truly amazing last night. When you played your song, I just had to sit down and have a cry. It was beautiful."

"Thank you," said Kjartan. "I just want to say thank you to all of you for coming here. For being obedient. For taking risks, for our sakes. Iceland is not the same place as it was three days ago. You have touched everyone. God has touched everyone through you."

He hugged Helena and the leaders, as the crowd clapped and cheered.

Joz came over and hugged him.

Jonathan stepped forward with Susan.

"I believe tonight is going to be powerful," said Jonathan.

"God says he is going to release his spirit in power," said Susan. "His power comes from his authority, his *kratos*. His power is also dynamic. That is *dunamis* power. He uses dunamis power when he does miracles through us."

"Let's get going with worship," said Jonathan. "There's an old song called Light The Fire Again. It's in my spirit. Can we begin with that one, please Jas?"

The band went up to their places. There was now an orchestra of local people in the area between the ring stage and the drums stage. They had screens set up in front of each player.

Jasper tapped his sticks and started drumming out the beat. The guitar players, including Joz and Archie came in. Mark did not know the song, but the hologram and the colours on his keyboard directed him on which chords to play. Imogen led the singing. Many of the children had joined her as backing singers.

The crowd clapped along. There was an atmosphere of joy and celebration.

The next song was more upbeat, about the happy day of salvation. Mark remembered it from the church in New Birmingham. Mark smiled when he spotted Archie. He was going for it on his electric guitar, bouncing along the stage.

When they got to the line, "you have saved me" the whole meeting shouted it out.

There was cheering and clapping from the crowd, as the song ended.

"Let's have some disco!" said Jasper and they played three songs that had many in the crowd dancing.

The Comms guys played on the crowd with the bright coloured lights and lasers. Mark had nice, simple parts to play on his keyboard.

Imogen sang, "Let your love shine all over the world" in one song.

In another song, the chorus went, "I feel happy now."

Many people in the crowd called out "Don't You Worry Child," so they did Mark's version again.

This time, for Mark, it was like surfing on a big wave. He did not feel alone. He felt like it was one huge party. He could not stop grinning when Rachel and Olina ran up onto the stage to dance with Imogen. Johnson and Sanjay came up and danced around him. The crowd sang with him. They were jumping up and down and dancing, as soon as the beat picked up.

At one point, between lines, he called out to the crowd,

"Let's hear you, Iceland!"

The response was another huge cheer that filled the dome.

The Comms guys made a moving grid with the lasers, over the heads of the crowd. Then they had more lasers coming out from a single point high up, so they made it seem like they were moving at speed. They made the space throb to the music. Mark loved it. He pointed at them, and gave them a big thumbs up. To his surprise, the place erupted with indoor fireworks.

They crowd made a loud noise to show their approval.

The smoke from the fireworks added to the effect of the lights.

The song finally ended.

"Now, one of our team had a dream last night," said Jasper. "God said he was going to give him a song. How about it, can we do it now?"

Mark nodded.

The spotlight was on him. He started with the first simple chords. The words came up on the screens as he sang.

"You are God, we are your creation
You are wise, while we were foolish
You are strong, while we were weak
You are patient, while we were hasty
You are humble, while we were proud
You are forever, while we live day by day."

Jasper came in with the drums. The band followed.

Imogen came over to him to sing the chorus with him. She knew it because Jasper had played it back to her earlier.

"You are my Lord
I am here, I am your child
I am yours, and you are mine
My Lord, my Father, my Redeemer and my Healer."

The band and the orchestra joined in with him for the second verse.

"You died so that we could live
We were caught, but you set us free
When you speak, we listen
When you teach, we learn
When you command, we obey
When you call, we answer
When you fill, we have joy
When you reveal, we understand
When you touch, we are healed."

This time everyone joined in with the chorus. Mark looked up to catch a glimpse of the crowd and the lights. The song ended with clapping and he waved.

"I hope you are going to love this next song," said Jasper. "It's called God's Great Dance Floor."

Mark started carefully with the first few chords. He had learnt this one that afternoon with Jasper.

Imogen and Archie sang together about going back to God's heart.

Then Jasper came in with the drums, and the guy on bass added a strong rhythm. Archie added a driving lead on his electric guitar.

The crowd were clapping and stamping their feet.

They sang about God always loving them, about the future beginning here and now. The music built into a crescendo. The Comms guys released more fireworks. Another cheer went up.

They kept repeating the line about feeling alive, coming alive, being alive.

There was a section just for the instruments.

"Do you feel alive?" Mark asked crowd.

There was a wall of response.

"Me too," he said grinning.

Mark felt carried along in the song, like on a strong tide. His heart felt immensely happy. They sang the chorus over and over. The whole room seemed to be pulsating with music, bodies and lights. A guy with a trumpet came up and played the solo.

At the end of the song, Jonathan came forward again.

"It is time to invite the Spirit of God to come," he said. "Are you ready?"

He stood with his hands outstretched wide.

"Holy Spirit, we invite you to come now. Fire of God, come!"

Mark had a good vantage point to see what happened next.

It seemed like a wave was moving around the space. It was like watching wind move over a field of wheat. As the wave moved, people were swaying, some falling. It went from the front to the back, all around the space.

Then laughter broke out with the wave. Wherever it moved, people started laughing loudly. Next, people were shaking and falling down. Some would try and get up again, only to be shaken again and collapsing, with more laughter.

"Fill them with joy," prayed Jonathan.

He waved an arm in one direction and all the people still standing in that direction, all keeled over. This produced more hysterical laughter. He waved another arm. More went over. He turned and waved towards the band. They all went down. Mark was holding onto his keyboard. He waved again and Mark slumped to the floor, laughing his head off and shaking.

"Be filled with the Spirit," called Jonathan.

Helena was trying to get up the stairs. He waved his arm towards her and she went down, shaking on the stairs, crawling back down.

"Get everyone at the back, Lord," he said. A wave went around the back rows of the tent. The people standing were bowled over like ninepins.

"Give them another blast," said Jonathan.

More waves of laughter went around the room.

Mark heard a deep rumbling sound, like an approaching train coming up from the lake. It seemed to be coming right towards the tent. The ground began to shake. The rumble kept up for some moments then it seemed to pass on out to the other side and the sound receded and the shaking ceased.

Mark had never experienced an earthquake before, but he felt completely safe.

When it was over, Jonathan prayed again.

"Thank you for what you have done here, Father. Seal every good work you have done in their hearts. Give them faith, hope and love. Lead them into truth. Teach them true worship.

Continue to heal their hearts. Give them joy. Amen."

The main meeting was over. Families with children departed. Many stayed to pray together. Many lying on the floor were still getting the laughter.

Mark joined the others on the coach back to the city. They were drained and feeling ready for sleep by the time they reached their berth.

As they were saying goodnight, Sanjay and Johnson said that both loved Mark's song.

"You know what? You are a true worshipper," said Sanjay.

"Thanks. Bless you both," replied Mark.

Soon they were all asleep.

In Mark's dream, he was playing in sunshine on a beach with friends.

DAY 15

The next day was spent packing up the site. They dismantled everything in reverse order. This time, there were numerous local people who willingly helped. The main tent came down gracefully and its sections were rolled up and loaded. Jan and Tomas strode around the site, giving instructions. Sanjay was kept busy, providing countless meals. They had another go on the catapult before it was taken down.

That evening, they had an early supper at The Harp.

When they came out, there was a large crowd to wave them off.

The Icelandic leader, who was called Hinrik, made a farewell speech.

"Please remember that you can visit us anytime. We will give you our best hospitality," he promised. "As you go, you must know that we can never thank you enough for what you have done here. We owe you a debt we cannot repay. We are your friends and your family. We bless you with a thousand blessings."

He embraced Jonathan and Helena and kissed them.

They all boarded the train and waved out of the open windows.

The train driver hooted and moved slowly off.

Some children ran alongside the carriage, waving and smiling until the train picked up speed.

Soon they were in the tunnel.

The team congregated in the lounge car as they had done on the way up. They shared stories and sang some songs. They did a folk music version of Mark's song.

Later on they washed and got ready for bed.

Mark felt a pleasant weariness. It had been hard work, but as fulfilling as he had imagined it would be.

They said goodnight.

There was a gentle sway to the movement of the train.

Mark drifted into a deep sleep.

In his dream, he was standing in the desert, as before, shading his eyes against the intense glare. There was the sandstorm: it filled the view from earth to sky: awesome, forbidding, intense. There were the steel discs spinning at frightening speed. Yet again, he was overwhelmed by the scale and power of the sandstorm. This time, words came to him, like an earnest message: *This is going to happen. The winds of change are coming.*

* * * * * *

Flashback Saturday 21st January 2017

The snow was falling in Davos.

The four friends were sitting together around a table, dressed for dinner.

"Are we agreed, the time has come?" asked the American.

"All is prepared," said the Indian.

"The world is about to experience chaos like it has never known," said the South African.

"There is a tide," said the Englishman, "in the affairs of men. Let us take the current."

The End

Acknowledgements and thanks

I have so many people to thank: my family, first and foremost.

My father imparted to me a love of the story and of words written well. His letters to me at school were witty, and as sharp as a blade. He would have made an exceptional academic. He died in 1993. I miss him.

My mother was our main nurturer and gave me a love of adventure.

My sister Liza is an author, and gave wise advice.

My stepmother Angelika was generous in her support.

Two people stand out in my school days with helping me in creative writing: Mrs. Jane Maclure, a demanding English teacher at prep school-if your writing was lazy, you soon heard about it; and Paul Watkins, a friend a year older than I in my house at school, he helped me see the potential in writing a story even with a simple title, like 'The Bench.' He is a talented author.

I came to Christian faith in Edinburgh, Scotland, aged 25. Many friends helped me in those early years: Roger Simpson, Roger Cooke, Pippa Rimmer, Kenny Macaulay, Cameron Collington, David Scott, Martin Williamson, Ray Dunn, James Croft, Eileen Kerr, Angie Inchley -to name a few.

I thank all the children I have had the privilege of teaching in the last ten years: I have learnt many things, including something of how you see the world.

In my current role, many have encouraged me and have been generous friends: Jonathan Perry, Jenny Perry, Morne Vosloo, Warren Miller, Caroline Miller, Rebecca Noon, Martyn Ford, Peter Thacker and many others.

Sincere thanks to my friends the Cavans for your love and advice.

Thank you to my proofreaders: Josh Menzies and Becky Williams.

Thank you to my script doctor: Mark Stibbe.

Thank you to Kim Cross and everyone at Grosvenor House Publishing.

I am deeply grateful to many worship leaders and musicians in the church for music that has lifted me and accompanied me on my walk over the years: love and blessing to you for helping me worship: Kent Henry, Kevin Prosch, World Wide Message Tribe, Ian White, Iona, Charlie Groves, Cathy Burton, Vineyard, Martin Smith and Delirious, Toby Mac, Matt Redman, Brenton Brown, Phatfish, Tim Hughes, Worship Central, Bethel, Hillsong United, Hillsong Young and Free, among others.

Lightning Source UK Ltd.
Milton Keynes UK
UKOW02f0652010716

277467UK00002B/9/P